DR. JOSEF'S LITTLE BEAUTY

DR. JOSEF'S LITTLE BEAUTY

a novel

ZYTA RUDZKA

Translated by

ANTONIA LLOYD-JONES

SEVEN STORIES PRESS
NEW YORK · OAKLAND

SEVEN STORIES PRESS
140 Watts Street
New York, NY 10013
www.sevenstories.com

College professors and high school and middle school teachers may order free examination copies of Seven Stories Press titles. Visit https://www.sevenstories.com/pg/resources-academics or email academic@sevenstories.com.

Library of Congress Cataloging-in-Publication Data is on file.

ISBN: 978-1-64421-375-9 (paperback)
ISBN: 978-1-64421-376-6 (ebook)

Printed in the USA

9 8 7 6 5 4 3 2 1

For Mama

The first time she stood before Dr. Josef, she was twelve years old and naked, and could sense his delight.

Powerful, attentive gaze. Hand clenched in a white glove. Steady strokes of the riding crop against his polished boots.

He had spotted her at once. Bony. Veinous. Sinewy. Face veiled in thick curls. Abdomen frost-coated. Calves crooked. Thighs a small bubble of winter air could squeeze between.

Standing in a group of hunchbacks, cripples, dwarves, and twins. Among children with deformed limbs that would be on display in a biology museum in just a few weeks' time. Next to them wailed some bonny babies, still warm from their mothers' arms. They showed him some Gypsy babies too, with lovely teeth and perfectly dome-shaped skulls that would adorn many a desktop after boiling. They would suit the silence of Berlin offices and libraries.

But he was looking only at her. They pushed her twin sister forward to join her. He flashed a glance at her. Different. He barely nodded and returned his gaze to her. He pointed his index finger to the right, anointing her as research material.

Again he examined her alone. He spared her no word or touch. His admiration was mute. He fondled with his gaze. He injured in his thoughts. Slid his eyes over her breasts. The breasts of a child. Cringing. With tiny nipples. Teats like early summer pale pink strawberries.

Suddenly he came near. One step. Two. He stood close. Stretched out a hand. Touched her with the crop. Her body buckled. The skin sagged into a small hollow. He pushed. It hurt. She didn't move. *Ja, gut*. He liked her.

He lowered the crop. She was different. She didn't cry. As if she couldn't feel the cold. Smell the odor. The stench of burning human flesh. She remained bored. Shifted from foot to foot. With her face grim. Tense. She carried out his orders. Knelt. Rose on tiptoes. Raised her arms. Turned around. Stood side on. Back facing. Leaned over. Straightened up. Chest forward. Looked him right in the eyes. That surprised him, but also amused him. Some hair was stuck to her lips, so she idly brushed it aside. As she did, she put her finger to her lips, as if bidding him be silent.

He was pleased. It was concentrated pleasure to be brought something like this.

He wanted to hurl her. Watch her fly. Onto the gravel. He gave her a mighty shove. She fell. Lay there. Arms spread wide. Legs apart. Pressed into the grit. But not dead yet. She shuddered. Moved. Stood up. Tensed. Wiped her face clean of the mucus secreted as she fell.

They all feared the summer, but no one spoke of it.

And now it was setting in. Gradually. Unhurriedly. Relentlessly. First there was a short, cool shower, but the grass soon shook off the dew. Then the sun flared more and more fiercely. Streams of bright light proliferated, conquering each shady area of the garden in turn.

The rodents moved out into the fields. The pungent smell of mouse urine wasn't so easily expelled from the dining room. The whitewashed tables were put outside. That was where they ate their meals now, lay down to rest, and waited for family visits. The terrace was paved with flagstones. Chipped. Weather-beaten. The odd blade of grass protruded from under them.

Helena took her first step. She moved cautiously, as if entirely shattered inside. Her head bounced dangerously, it didn't fit her body, but looked as if forcibly planted onto her limp neck. As she walked, she watched the other residents. Sitting on the terrace. Staring into space. Basking in the sunshine like lizards, static among stones. Presenting themselves to be bathed in warmth. Skulls thinly coated in sparse, dry hair. Faces like several pieces of skin sewn together. Cheeks marked with bruises, wounds and suppurating scratches. Tissue-paper eyelids. Bellies swollen by disease. Furrowed hands. Gnarled fingers. Ruffled thighs. Hanging loose. Wobbling with every motion of the body. Feet liberated from bootees and slippers. Large, misshapen toes. Growths. Lumps. Watery tumors.

It looked as if they were waiting for something. They stared at the entrance gate for hours on end. By noon it was hard to see, dissolving in the blazing heat of the sun, blurring amid the rusty railings. The tarnished wicket seemed eternally shut. As if it were a stage prop through which no one ever exited. Beyond which nothing existed.

Helena stopped. She groped for a jug of warm liquid. Her fingers wound around a glass. She gripped it the way someone whose head is spinning leans against a wall. She narrowed her rheumy eyes.

The flower boxes were filled with annuals. Rubber plants trapped in clay pots had been brought into the fresh air. Their fleshy, meaty leaves towered over the lawn. Old vine shoots gave way to young green ones, quickly covering the high fence that bordered the property.

Last year's sun umbrellas had been dusted off. Deck chairs, plastic armchairs, and little camping tables had been set out on the terrace.

Ah, so here comes another June, she said quietly, to herself.

She sat down for a moment. Took out her powder puff. Tidied a curl above her ear. Took a long look at herself in a small oval mirror. She was proud of her smooth complexion. If she'd chosen to wear glasses, she'd have noticed a dense network of fine incisions on her cheeks, like paper cuts. She looked like a doll with a porcelain face from an antique shop.

I forgot to tell you, folks, said her twin sister, Leokadia. She had a childlike voice.

Listen, yesterday a ladybug sat on my skirt. A wonderful little ladybug . . . And on the radio they said there are meadows with thirty-eight varieties of wild orchid and twenty species of bee. Isn't that wonderful?

She smiled, showing her brown gums.

After a long pause she spoke again:

Can you feel it? It's summer, isn't it? Time to be off to the allotment garden. Everything that's alive is buzzing, bustling, blooming. Dear Mother Nature is dressing herself up for us. As if in a day or two she were due to celebrate an important occasion. A wonderful event. Just look, isn't it lovely here? . . . You see, Helena? You're glad, aren't you? Yesterday it was two years since we came here, we had a cry, but today we're managing to be happy again. How wonderful . . . Spring is over, but it's still so beautiful here.

She looked all around. Her chin was quivering.

I couldn't agree with you more, Leokadia. We are most fortunate, said Henryk, nodding.

He was almost eighty. Puffy, bloated, with an egg-shaped skull covered in the remains of hair, and liver spots showing through.

We can enjoy some recreation. Get some fresh air. Be on holiday to our heart's content, he gushed.

He glanced at the caretaker standing by the garden toolshed. His figure looked heavy, motionless as an obelisk. Then he glanced at Helena. Showing off her slender legs in a wine red pantsuit. Beside her, Leokadia. Hiding beneath a thin crêpe dress with a low-cut, frilly neckline, over which she had thrown a shawl patterned with yellow primulas.

Henryk smiled at his own thoughts. From the sisters' clothes one could tell that summer was here. They had dropped the dark colors. Leokadia's little felt hat had been replaced by a straw model with a wavy brim, and Helena was more eager to wear her hair loose.

They were always impeccably dressed. Even at table they never removed their elegant gloves. They had pale, as if aristocratic faces. Henryk had a weakness for pale women. Although Leokadia would sometimes turn brick-red, which came with tiring blood-pressure surges. Moreover, her looks were marred by her nose, which had such a prominent bone—one more grimace and it would pierce the skin.

Helena was more refined. Fragile. Her face a subtle oval. Her dark eyes ever narrowed, perhaps sensitive to the light.

And she still had the profile that Dr. Josef had once admired. Sometimes he had touched it. Stroked her long hair, gathering it back to form a rich cape. Stroked her conical breasts. Fingered the spot where soon after his assistant would inject brown liquid taken from her ulcerating forearm.

Now Helena no longer had that forearm. Her empty sleeve ended in the side pocket of her pantsuit. It had been photographed each week. In the hospital barrack. While taking blood from her ear. On a stretcher in natural light. Dr. Josef was proud of his photograph collection. He documented his long months of research, proving that human material didn't go to waste.

Can you smell the sea, my dears? asked Henryk, sitting up in his chair.

Yes, a distinct breeze, he said, and glanced at Helena, seeking confirmation.

A faint puff of fresh air. A palpable hint of the sea. Salt particles. Iodine, iodine, can you smell it? he kept asking, running his tongue over his rough lips. Chapped, as if by a layer of sea salt.

Can you smell the sea? he said, smacking his lips in jubilation.

They didn't answer.

They were looking forward to cherries. Their thoughts were of cherries, in bedrooms, the common room, the treatment room, on the terrace and in corridors. They'd mention them while walking around, resting, queuing for a bath. Getting bored. Taking their temperature. Awaiting their families. Suffering. Looking at the roses and anemones in vases.

They talked of nothing but cherries. Each person's favorites: large with thin skin, small, sweet, watery. Stringy, tart, like sour cherries. Or light, white or also dark, purple, fleshy, almost mealy. Pretty, compact, a pity to eat them. Shapeless, pecked by starlings, gone bad, too moldy to eat, like a bitter, watery bladder. With tiny stones, flimsy peel. Or else huge, hard, well-padded with pulp, enveloping all the sweetness.

From time to time Henryk savored the memory of the mangoes he'd eaten in Africa. He'd describe the thick, sickly-sweet juice slowly trickling down his chin. But they always shouted him down: Cherries, our cherries.

Each person wanted to tell about the ones they'd had in childhood. The men boasted of the high trees they'd climbed. Quickly. Barefoot. Knees hugging a rebellious trunk. How they'd picked the fruits from the very top, while the branches shook, bending to the ground. The women fondly remembered twin cherries. They'd hooked them on their ears. Worn them with pride, like ruby earrings.

They wouldn't let each other speak. Each one wanted to be heard. Once, long ago, they had eaten the best, the most wonderful cherries. From Grandma's basket. From Grandpa's rough hands. From Momma's lips. From Father. From a lover. A fiancé. A newly married wife. A stranger.

They were looking forward to their cherries. But meanwhile the dessert bowls were full of strawberry compote, rhubarb crumble, pear fool, and over-stewed apples sprinkled with cinnamon.

Nature was in a rare state of animation.

If you set an ear to it, the earth was rumbling with the sound of roots splitting clods streaked by snails. Plants were burgeoning in all directions. And there were flowers everywhere. New ones every day. Petals were unfurling, receiving more and more sunlight. Stamens were shaking off their yellow dust. The flower beds, plots, and patches sparkled with color, then paled in the midday sun. Couch grass boldly took possession of every rut in the footpath.

O Stanisław Kostka, saintly youth in heaven, prayed Benia quietly.

Among the angels you brightly shine. You stand by the throne of the Virgin Mary. For your innocence is sublime, she whispered. Her lips opened. And closed with unusual precision. Her large, toilworn hands barely touched each other in her gesture of prayer.

I pray for my late husband, Staś. And in life's final hours, may we merit a death like yours, O holy youth now glorified, taken to Our Lady's side. O patron of our Polish race, protect us from the devil, beseech the Virgin full of grace to keep our youth from evil.

Benia fell silent, putting a medallion of the Virgin Mary to her lips.

Helena watched her until she felt an intense pain in her hip.

Dragging her leg, she turned back to the home.

She sat down on a bench beside Leon. He rarely came out to take the air. He often sat by his palm tree. It was too large for his room; it had been placed in the corridor, so that if his door was open, he could keep an eye on it. He never abandoned it. If he had to go to the treatment room or for a bath, he'd pay someone to guard his plant.

How quiet it is here. Out on the terrace there's always somebody moaning, asking for water or worst of all—reminiscing. But here it's divinely quiet, declared Helena, to get the conversation going.

To her distaste, she noticed that Leon had fixed his glasses frame with a soiled band-aid again.

How quiet it is, she repeated.

Yes, there's a distinct lack of sound waves in the air, agreed Leon. And stopped his heavy glasses from slipping off his nose with an index finger.

You have such an odd way of putting things. Once you described the cleaner's child as an adult at the initial stage, said Helena, laughing.

I wouldn't call that a faithful quotation. But so be it, he agreed.

I'm told you've had a difficult life? she asked. She gazed ahead, opening and closing her eyes as if in slow motion. The hot weather was causing them to redden and water more than usual.

A difficult life is nothing more than the absence of an easy life. That's all, said Leon, chuckling.

And that's nothing to fear. Think about it now and then. But not on an empty stomach. That sort of meditation has a disastrous effect on the digestion.

He gasped for breath after a moment of mirth.

How quiet it is. On the whole I don't like being here anymore. It's like being in the grave, sighed Helena.

And regretted it instantly. She regarded sighing as an old person's weakness.

Yes, there's a lack of sound waves in the air, repeated Leon.

He leaned to the right and blew on the palm leaves. Motes of dust swirled around them.

Ever since I've lived here I've felt as if I were sitting on train tracks, watching an engine approaching.

There was a long pause before he replied.

Are you anxious?

I don't know. It's this kind of confinement. I know it, and I hate it, she answered, stretching out a leg and examining her shoe.

He looked at her.

Well, there's no hiding the fact that this isn't the easiest place to live. Especially for those gifted with an unusual aesthetic sense. But ugliness is nothing more than an absence of beauty. And a pong is the dark side of a perfume. For individuals like you it's not easy to live in such places. But paradoxically, despite the daily deficiencies, it's the people like you who survive the longest.

But I don't want to survive here. And certainly not the longest, said Helena indignantly.

I don't want to be here, do you see? Every day I call my stepdaughter to get her to take me away from here. I ask the manager, the nurses, the caregivers, the delivery men. Even the priest. Everyone. Everyone. I insist on it. Take me away. I'm not one of these dribbling idiots. Someone who comes into the common room dressed in nothing but dirty diapers. Or one of the lucky ones deprived of memory. No, I am not. Look at me, please. I'm in full possession of my faculties, as they say. I'm in full possession of my intellectual, physical, and all other faculties. I look very well. I've always taken care of myself. But here they make fun of me. This isn't a beauty parlor, Helena. They cackle. And when I asked for tonic to cleanse my face because nothing but chlorine pours from the faucet, Miron laughed out loud: Helena, steel yourself. Tomorrow they'll be delivering mineral water. Straight from the Styx. From the Styx, just imagine. That bumpkin. Where did he get that word from? I bet he never had higher education. Technical college at best.

Helena broke off. She opened her purse and briefly rummaged in it. She took out a ballpoint. She pretended to be lighting it with a lighter. She acted as if inhaling.

After a while she spoke:

I'm sorry, I'm calm now. A lady shouldn't show her feelings. But some of the residents sure can get on my nerves.

She inhaled again.

Nice plant, she added without interest, out of politeness.

It's *Licuala grandis*, explained Leon.

A very fine specimen. Almost ten foot. Quite hard to cultivate. If you don't love it, of course. It likes to be in a warm spot, but not in direct sunlight. They want to put it in the chapel—over my dead body. No, not even over my dead body. The Sisters of Saint Elizabeth have promised that when I die they'll take it to their canteen. *Licuala grandis* requires moist air. It has to be given lukewarm boiled water. And misted. One of the caregivers has not just a special knack for it but also a tender heart, said Leon in a softened tone.

He took a close look at Helena's face. She seemed to him too garishly made-up.

When I was to come here from home, all I took was this.

Helena paused.

Gripping her purse beneath her stump, with the surviving hand she tossed the pen into it. She took out a plastic bag. For a moment she wondered whether to reveal her secret. Finally she raised her hand to display the contents of the bag more clearly. Inside it, various documents, cards and notelets were visible.

Bills. You see? Old bills for gas, electricity, and rent too. Quite a pile over all the years. I can't throw them out. I simply can't. Eccentricity, true. And my husband, a qualified engineer, he was always in a suit for dinner. It's nice, your little palm tree.

Licuala grandis. I grew it from a seed. It didn't fit in my room. It has sloped ceilings, you see. So they put it here. It's a good thing the corridors are tall. They wanted to take it to the chapel. Or the common room. They were adamant. Only the manager didn't care. And I like to be close to my *Licuala grandis*. I wrote an appeal and I won. You have to fight for your rights. Especially when you love something.

We miss you on the terrace, Leon.

I have to guard it. Despite its impressive size, *Licuala grandis* is highly sensitive, quite defenseless. Are you aware of the fact that the residents relieve themselves into the plant pot? I can understand them having problems to do with disorders of the urinary system, but one should maintain at least some good manners and a degree of human dignity in any circumstances.

I understand, I understand perfectly. I too am sensitive to whether someone is a gentleman or a cad. Just from the way he opens his mouth to speak. He doesn't have to say anything. The movement of the lips is enough for me, agreed Helena, adjusting her pant leg.

The leaves wither and curl, explained Leon, looking at the palm.

Licuala grandis is very fragile. It's not at home here. They're like emigrants. Far from their own land, their own sun. That's why they have to have special treatment. It's harder for them. And just imagine: now and then some caregiver with a primitive, thoughtless personality opens the window. And at once there's a draft. My *Licuala grandis* starts wilting visibly. The leaves start curling. Losing vigor. And on top of that they urinate into the pot. Can you imagine? Some of the residents can't tell a plant pot from a urinal. Like dogs. Though I'm very fond of dogs. Straight into the plant pot. Like dogs.

Helena shielded her mouth with her hand.

Apparently none of the residents has just secondary education. It seems everyone went to college too, she said.

No one has just secondary education, that's what my sister assured me. Because I didn't want to come here. Not in the least. I was lonely, but I had misgivings. That's how she persuaded me. She said I'd finally have my sort of company in here. But there's nobody here but louts, boors, simpletons, bumpkins, dimwits, clods, dopes, boneheads, birdbrains, dunces, jackasses, you get the idea? Numskulls and nincompoops.

I'm not imagining it, Helena. Straight into the plant pot, repeated Leon. And immediately added:

In the past I had a wild streak too. At the student dorm I used to piss in the washbasin and cut my toenails on the table top. Let's not be afraid to bring up our own youthful impudence. Did your husband piss in the washbasin too?

No. As far as I know, he did not. No, it's impossible. He wasn't tall enough.

My wife was tiny too. Pocket-sized. Like a little Chinese pillow made of sumptuous, stylish silk. You didn't feel the urge to listen to her or speak to her. What you wanted was to touch her, caress and stroke her. Feel her skin beneath your fingertips, run your hand over it. She was like a figurine of an eastern idol that brings good luck when you touch it. You're sure to be familiar with the sort of women who are easy on the eye. You're one of them yourself.

Thank you for the compliment. An appreciation of someone else's values and virtues is a genuine rarity in this company. Scoundrels. Mediocrities. You must have loved your wife very much.

It's impossible to hide. Although talking about my feelings is not my domain.

Leon took a deep breath, making his cheeks sink and the veins on his temples swell.

My husband was a very decent man, declared Helena.

He died. I wept, though mourning did me good, I can't complain. Black suits me. But I'd like to have more of life. Walk around parks and fields. Have someone carry me in his arms like a lamb. Hug me. Or hold hands. You're probably not too shocked by that. Please understand, I don't want to be a widow for the rest of my life. I am not one of the kind to rattle off their prayers, to sit plucking feathers and gossiping, or reminisce. When I can't sleep I have such wonderful reveries. I can see it. It's there before my eyes. As if it were real. I'm getting married again. I'm wearing beautiful make-up. My hair is elegantly backcombed. It looks like a golden halo, making my face seem extremely interesting. Genuinely healthy. I'm wearing a dress of refined silk lace, and a veil of tulle. My bridegroom is laughing out loud. He's so happy. Oh, Our Lord in heaven has often wagged his finger at me from on high and said: Helena, don't make me come down there.

Leon nodded a few times.

It's true that a certain kind of reverie really can anesthetize a person against all suffering and hardship. Dreaming while awake, that's the healthiest form of hibernation when we're bothered by reality.

My husband was a qualified engineer, said Helena, interrupting him.

My wife was a biology teacher. She was very fond of dogs. There was always a dog at home. So whenever I stroke a dog it's as if life, my old life with my wife, were still happening. The caretaker has a sheepdog, but he doesn't come with him anymore. He was banned by the manager. The residents were afraid he would jump up at them and knock them over. But I think he was too gentle for that. Why won't they let him in? He used to fawn, pushing his muzzle against your hand to be stroked. How he loved to retrieve a ball. Did you see how I used to play with him? I was always smuggling something from lunch for him. He sat so politely. Never once did he raise his paws to the plant pot.

Leon, I must be frank and say that I don't like the barking of dogs. As soon as I hear it I feel pain. Everything comes back to me. The prison guards. The yapping of sheepdogs. As if I were being undressed. My lovely dresses ripped off. I feel like howling.

She broke off to take a breath.

She went on:

My husband was a qualified engineer. I've told you that, Leon, huh? Haven't I? she asked indifferently. She was trying to calm down.

My wife was interested in butterflies, he said.

For a few moments they sat in silence.

Leon ran his fingertips over the plant's stem.

Helena watched the residents trailing aimlessly down the corridor. She had noticed that the first burst of heat had caused them all to be seized by an idle melancholy. They were moldering. Persistently bored. They shuffled along wearily. As if straight off the train. After a long trip. They often stopped to rest their bodies against their walking frames. Slowly, almost imperceptibly, they were slumping. Something was pulling them toward sleep. Snatching their wakefulness. They were nodding off, hanging onto the frame. Then they awoke—without surprise, and shambled onward.

After my husband's funeral I bought myself some red lipstick, said Helena.

I painted my lips. And wore my prosthesis again. As you can see, my left forearm is missing. Long ago, in the early 1960s, straight after the compensation, my husband managed to get me a good German prosthesis. I didn't like to put it on. Although he begged me to. Why was I so stubborn? I lost my arm several years after the camp. Something went wrong with it. There'd always been problems with it. Dr. Josef singled it out for himself. If it had come off in the camp, they'd have given me more money. The war was long over, but it went on suppurating. I tried poultices, infusions, various ointments. Even those ones of my sister's, made of all sorts of herbs. Nothing helped. And suddenly there was gangrene, so they took it off.

She fell into thought, then spoke up again:

But on the whole I love being alive. Though after the camp, you know, somehow I couldn't get back to complete normality. My husband went to great trouble to get me a German prosthesis. And it's very nice. Flesh-colored. As if suntanned. It even behaves like a real hand. It can pass things, deal cards, caress, or make a fist. The Germans know how to disassemble a person and then reassemble them.

She fell silent.

I called my wife "my little bit of bread," nice, huh? We met a good few years after the war. I was behind the wire from forty-two, but nobody ever knew. Not even my wife. I renounced my childhood. I used to say I'd forgotten it all. That I'd been raised in the countryside, by good peasants. I abandoned everything. I even denied my family, my dead. Out of fear. I never said a thing. Not once. She didn't ask questions. I studied physics. I was taught that life is a chaotic system. Impossible to plan. Or predict. A minor disturbance can double in two days, a thousandfold in twenty, and a billion times in two months. I researched chaos, I preferred to furnish my mind with that sort of thing only. Theories, hypotheses, anything except the past.

Helena tidied her hair.

It took Leon a while to find the right words:

Only now am I able to talk to them, he declared, gazing at the palm.

Only now am I able to talk to them. To my dead. I simply ask them to expect me. To be waiting. Not to be afraid anymore. After all, metal rusts, timber burns. So do we, and that's that.

Helena noticed how small he was.

She wanted to hug him, but she couldn't. She had never hugged anyone. Not even her sister, her husband, or herself.

The caregivers kept the residents company with evident detachment.

With the ill-concealed politeness typical of bored lackeys. They served mint tea seasoned with raspberry sweetener and rather stale cookies.

Diluted sounds rose over the terrace, as if wrapped in warm wool: the noise of plates being laid, the anemic clink of teaspoons against mugs, the trickle of tea.

Despite a light, mixed diet the food was an ordeal. Half-heartedly, lethargically, the residents moved their mouths. They looked as if forced to raise the forks and spoons, to chew and swallow. They ate out of necessity, to kill time or to keep faith with themselves after eating for so many years. It was as if they had no appetite, no sense of taste or smell, or pleasure from being together at table. They didn't talk to each other. They slurped, broke wind, wheezed, and belched. They clumsily grappled with the false teeth that slipped as they worked their jaws.

Sniff the air. It smells of summer now, doesn't it? It would have been time to go to the allotment garden, said Leokadia, hiding a piece of bread in her cuff.

You've got a garden here, drawled Miron. Wiry, shriveled, with lips that only moved on the right side.

He spat out a half-chewed sandwich beside his plate. He looked as if his head were hanging on a hook.

Irritated, Henryk groped the table top in search of a fork.

I hereby declare that I've put in a request not to have breakfast with you anymore.

His watery eyes were goggling, dominating his swollen yellow face. His gaze was foggy, faded, an attribute of the poor-sighted.

Must you check the contents of your oral cavity after crushing up your food? he asked in a softened tone.

Miron clenched his lips. He stopped moving. A spasm crossed his face, to be replaced at once by a gentle smile.

Yet he replied:

Not everyone's memory is good enough for him to know what he's put in his gob.

Henryk battled the weariness flooding his entire body, and forced himself to say:

Don't you start boasting. I have an atypical illness. I brought it back from Africa. From Africa. I was posted there. But where you're concerned diplomacy's not enough. A radical approach would have to be applied. For now I'm just warning. Giving good advice. If you go on practicing that senile ritual, they'll send you to our lakeside branch.

Miron laughed quietly and said:

A diplomatic note. Cigars rolled on the thighs of virgins.

He used his fingers to examine the contents of the mush beside his plate. His manner of speaking, fast and nervous, did not fit with his haggard body, almost entirely lacking muscles.

Eat. Eat up, insisted Benia, whose shrunken face was lacquered by a liverish complexion. Despite the heat wave she was wearing several tops and a knitted vest consisting of multicolored squares. Her flared skirt revealed her knees and was weighed down by an overstuffed pocket. In it she carried a shabby calendar with torn-off pages, a jar of gooseberry jam, stones removed from her gallbladder wrapped in plastic, and the petals that she spent the greater part of the day picking.

I gave birth to children. The cutest little babbies. The pinkest in the whole ward, she mumbled.

The boy weighed ten pounds. He was born blue, but he caught up, he soon caught up. Now he sells farm machinery. But not tractors, no, not tractors. Carrying the baby girl made me ugly. Mother of God, my whole face was covered in pimples. But not dry ones, no. Bunged up and weeping. That told me at once it was going to be a girl. But not tractors, no, not tractors.

She fell silent. Her mouth remained half open.

Her right leg was shorter, like a stringy stalk: shriveled and brown. She struggled to get under the table. Down on all fours, she picked up crumbs from breakfast. Whatever the time of year or day, she always went about in winter boots edged in sheepskin. As if she were afraid of a chill or frostbite. Something that had happened in the past.

Miron leaned forward, making it look as if any moment now his skull would break through the skin. As if he would fall over. With an open hand he rolled the spat-out mush:

Cigars rolled on the thighs of virgins. That's the life I had. Fancy handmade cigars.

Henryk wheezed. He was looking for flatware in his pants pocket.

Finally he emitted a plangent, childish lament:

Tomorrow I'll ask to be transferred to the table next to the nurses. They all eat in a decent manner there. They haven't forgotten what a knife and fork are for. This anti-intellectual atmosphere will drive me to the grave.

He broke off. His hand was stuck in the torn material lining his pants. He'd plainly come upon something interesting, because the quivering, milk-white rim of smooth hair marking the outer limit of his bald patch stopped moving.

Benia was trying to emerge from under the table, but lacked the strength.

There she sat, staring at Miron's boots. Misshapen, stiff, laced above the ankle. Coming from under the table, her voice seemed even more muffled:

My little girl visits me. Because my son's in America.

She whimpered softly. More and more softly.

Farm machinery, but don't tell me they're tractors. Tractors, she whispered.

But you said your granddaughter comes to visit, it's your daughter who's in America.

Helena was picking a slice of bread to pieces with her fingernails. Before swallowing, she kept them in her mouth to soak them in saliva.

Yes, my baby daughter, my little girl, my lovely little granddaughter. I wonder if she wants to be burned or buried? asked Benia in a weary tone.

Breathing heavily, she clambered out from under the table. She sat down on a chair. She sprinkled specks of bread onto an empty plate and set about separating them from accidentally gathered specks of earth, gravel, blades of grass, and hairs.

Cigars rolled on the thighs of virgins, squawked Miron.

His face took on a derisive expression. The mockery masked pain.

Henryk moved in his chair:

Africa. Africa. Baboons with dog's heads. Coconuts. If you sat beneath a palm tree, you had to make sure they didn't smash your head. Ferns with warts like fists. That was the life. I lived it to the full. Baboons. But that's all I remember. Baboons. What can you do. Mental blanks. Amnesia.

Dementia. Dementia.

Miron instantly corrected him.

Dementia. Dem—

He broke off, and took a deep breath.

Cigars rolled on the thighs of virgins. Cigars rolled on the thighs of virgins. Cigars roll—

He fell silent.

Leokadia was trying not to look at the curd cheese. At the snow-white mound that she couldn't easily hide in her cuff. At worst, she'd force it down her throat, and then vomit into one of the baskets lined with plastic bags that stood in the shower room.

She used to do that often. She'd eat herself full, for show, before her husband, or guests. Then she'd run straight to the bathroom and stick her fingers down her throat. She'd examine what she brought up. She'd spend some time inspecting it. Carefully. She was interested in everything that had been inside her.

Straight after that, exhaustion would come over her, sudden and violent. She'd run to bed, dive into the tangled bedding, pull her knees up under her chin, cover her head with a pillow, and shield her ears. She'd sleep, wheezily, warily, for barely fifteen minutes. Just as now, when she awoke, feeling Henryk's elbow nudging her arm.

The volunteer is coming to see to our feet, said Henryk.

He ran his gaze over the residents. He breathed in, to a point of pain. At such solemn moments he looked as if his ribs were about to crack, as if his skeleton were made of wicker.

But he continued:

In the circumstances I would like to stress that one should decide against this treatment. If my memory is not mistaken, according to an unwritten rule of this home, any resident who is no longer capable of cutting his own toenails is ranked just in front of one who cannot hold his urine. And poor bladder control is placed just behind brown gums and prostate. What's the danger? The danger of being evicted to the house by the lake. And that's all, my dears. I shan't say any more. The house by the lake. You know what that means.

He orated, while trying to extract his trapped hand. And moaned, while exhaling wheezily. His face swelled. His moist eyes were hidden in folds of skin.

Apparently at dawn someone else passed on? asked Leon.

He glanced at them as if at strangers. With a look of horror.

But they were listening to Miron. Struggling to put the words together, he spoke:

Those nurses of ours are all so feeble. Yesterday I fell off my chair, no big deal, huh? It can happen to anyone. But those bimbos just stood over me. Spineless creatures. So I'm lying there waiting, while they argue about who's going to lift me. I'd have got up by myself, but I was thinking: I'm coughing up my entire pension, so let them do the lifting. Finally I say: Ladies, I need help. Will one of you make a move? And they start running their mouths at me. Those bimbos. To them we're carrion with fat wallets. That's all.

Miron, if you want help, why not ask for it the right way, remarked Helena. Leokadia added:

I am really proud of our caregivers. They tell me so much. They read. They say what's going on in the world. They shake out my wig. They show me photos of their fiancés. They help me to dust my souvenirs. I'm eager for their news from outside. I'm not afraid of youth. I give our caregivers very special treatment, very special. There's so much to be learned from them, how to live and go on being a woman. A woman, not a skivvy. I can see I went along with my husband far too much. As if I had tacked myself onto him. But why? What for?

There was no one to defend me against my husband, chimed in Benia. And added:

But I taught my daughter to bite back.

Leokadia adjusted her dentures and said:

Things are different now. Once a person has clambered onto the springboard to death, they see things differently too. Even their own youth. What can I pass on to them, those caregivers of ours? A secret recipe for quince jam. Or how to ply your needle to make cross-stitch embroidery look nice.

She nodded.

The caregivers are as thin as whippets. One's just like another, muttered Miron, sticking to his guns.

Once upon a time a woman had what it took. Cigars rolled on the thighs of virgins. The manager has no taste at all. And the nurses are even worse, because—

He broke off to inspect the oatmeal more thoroughly.

I have so many things to pass on to my grandson. Did you know that children under twelve aren't able to visit us? A scandalous rule, added Henryk.

What can anyone learn from us? We lived in a different world, insisted Leokadia.

A person has one sacred right before death: to talk his heart out, proclaimed Henryk.

What is there to talk about? muttered Miron.

One thing I do know: living too long makes the heart change into a muscle. More than that: into a flabby muscle, declared Henryk.

Miron was slowly brightening up. But after a short while, he contentedly began to mix the mush with a fork. His wrist moved ponderously, counter-clockwise.

I don't want to reminisce, said Helena, slurping.

Everyone says this is a good time for reminiscence, but not for me.

Let's be glad we won't die young, laughed Miron.

I can't believe that of our entire family only Leolka and I will die in bed, between clean sheets, said Helena, tidying her hair.

All these silly little caregivers. All these silly little staff members. I have property. I demand the esteem due to my age and experience. It's professionalism that counts, not tits, offloaded Henryk wheezily.

He was close to tears because of his trapped hand. His eyelid was quivering.

Miron gripped his fork tighter, rocking his bowl. Just then he said angrily:

That bimbo pricked me badly. Caused a bruise across half my thigh. Lucky I can't see my butt. 'Cos I don't know what I'd do to hers.

It's not easy, not easy, Leon orated, gazing ahead:

My whole life was in a rush. But now it's at a standstill. As if one had sat down beside one's packed cases and were waiting and waiting. For God knows what. Surely not for death? Not yet. All these months. I've been waiting and waiting. And it's not coming. But what is not coming, my friends? he asked timidly. Benignly. As if afraid of the answer.

Briefly he stared at Benia's jam-stained nose. Then he closed his eyes. The pain was as sharp as if someone had pressed their knuckles into his eye sockets.

His bushy eyebrows rested on his spectacle frames and protruded above the lenses. Some of the hairs, coarse and straggling, brushed the arch of his nose. His face was puffy and red. As if squashed by something from one side. He wore old, drooping pants, over which he had sloppily pulled on a shirt. Once white, now going yellow. It exuded a smell of urine left by inadequate washing.

Instead of all those pills to increase the appetite they could serve better food, said Henryk.

To his own surprise, he had found peace. He'd hit on the idea of eating with his left hand.

They stint on our food. What's become of our balanced diet? They forget about the fibers in the leguminous vegetables. But the bowels are of top importance, he added in a weary tone.

They give us old cheeses, announced Miron, clearing his throat after each word.

And Henryk added:

Yet at a certain age one should take strict care of bowel function.

He winced, and wiped his mouth with the back of his hand.

I still have my old sense of smell, croaked Miron.

That yellow one stinks worse than— Well, I don't know what it's called. The kind that's for— That you put in a vase, in order to—

He froze. It looked as if he were dozing with his eyes open.

Eat, eat up. If only I could make you liver and apples! Finger-licking good, assured Benia.

She got up. She started walking from the table to the balustrade, from the balustrade to the table, there and back. She crossed those few yards hastily, taking tiny little steps, like a sewing needle.

Suddenly she stopped. She fixed her gaze on something. Stayed like that for quite a time, then toddled to her chair and sat down. She bowed her head to see what she had on her plate. She tried to straighten up, but couldn't, and hung dangerously over the edge of her glass.

Today someone crapped in my bed, exclaimed Miron, waking from his lethargy.

You should report it at once. They yelled at me about a stool that was lying under my quilt all day, advised Henryk.

His left hand was shaking too hard to send the fork to his mouth without mishap. He sucked in the yellow cheese.

I reported it. So what?

Miron seemed irritated, but also sad.

And that bimbo with the long hair said I'd crapped myself. And that it was just the same yesterday and the day before. That's slander. An insult. Blatant injustice. I don't recall anything of the kind.

He wanted to shout. He couldn't. His voice cracked. His spoon fell to the floor.

The caregivers have hearts of gold. But they have a hard time with us, said Leokadia, combing a strand of hair behind her ear with a fork.

Those mean bimbos. They screw us over. And the manager believes everything they say.

Miron was trying to speak loudly. His hand slyly crept over to steal Benia's spoon. She whimpered softly. Like a puppy taken from its mother.

That blonde, the one who failed to get into medical school, gave me a wash yesterday. I overheard her muttering: Come on, you old crone, quick march, get in the tub. That's why I don't like taking a bath. I'd rather give myself a nice sponge-off, said Benia, adjusting her lacy collar.

Who cares about an old boy like me? I stink of history, said Henryk, tired out by chewing. Laboriously he crammed the words between successive gulps of air:

I feel as if I've been caught in a snare. An old animal reeking of excrement. They used to bow to me. Waist deep. Africa. The service. Women with knees like ebony. Why on earth did I come back. At all. Why am I here. Anyway.

Benia interrupted him:

The nurses are no better either. The one in glasses called me a whale, or something of the kind. Yes, more like those African animals. And the one who's pregnant—

She pointed toward the caregivers.

She called me names, the one who's pregnant. A whale in soiled panties, that's what she said. I called my momma right away and told her everything. Everything. She said that when she gets here she'll give them a rough ride.

Our moms are dead. How do you call them? asked Szymon.

He was chewing a roll thoroughly, but only on one side of his jaw. Frothy saliva hung from his lips with crumbs of food stuck to it.

As a matter of fact, how did you make that call? They don't let us make calls. To anyone. So how did you do it? inquired Henryk, whistling like a kettle before releasing steam.

Miron spat oatmeal into Benia's hair:

But they've made this horrible. This is meant to be breakfast?

I call whenever I want, announced Benia proudly.

With the tip of her tongue she licked gooseberry jam from the jar.

Leokadia stopped the bread from slipping out of her sleeve. And declared:

Today, my dears, it's definitely impossible to make any calls. Somebody has peed on the phone in the caregivers' room again.

I call whenever I want, repeated Benia in the tone of a stubborn child:

I call when I get the desire. It comes over me, and I call at once.

She came to a stop, almost in tears.

Are there no cooks in this town, or what? Is this supposed to be food?

Miron scrutinized the vegetable mush.

Looks crummy, colorless, you see that? And as for flavor—like paper. And the portions are tiny. What is this stuff?

Purée, replied Benia. She leaned forward, sniffed, and added:

That's purée, can't you see? My kids were very happy with purée. Especially the kind at pre-school.

She came to a stop.

She began to pluck at the hairs on her chin.

Miron huffed:

Purée, that's a good one. I can see they've just pulped everything they had. But what they've gotten their hands on in that kitchen, only the health department can tell. If they ever move their asses and march over here. What the fuck am I saying? The guys from the health department would also like us to kick the bucket pronto.

Wine-red blotches covered Miron's face.

It's like with sausage, you want to eat it, but you don't want to know how they made it, declared Henryk.

Look here, folks, if you'd be so kind, would you call this a proper helping to feed a man? A distinguished diplomat? It's enough to make the cat laugh. Like a fly to feed a dog. I pay, and I have demands. I have demands. I have property.

He came to a stop. He laughed slyly. His brow was damp with sweat.

Like a fly to feed a dog, he repeated. He wiped the back of his head. He became goggle-eyed, as if he'd lost focus.

Eat up, eat. If only I could make you my liver and apples! Finger-licking good, whimpered Benia.

She was staring at a large wart on Miron's nose, which bobbed up and down as he spoke. Like an insect.

At the post I ate such a good salmon quiche that—recalled Henryk.

Like poetry. The sheer lyricism of daily life. An ode in culinary form.

A turd in culinary form. A turd, remarked Miron.

And spinach mousse in a lemon-and-pepper sauce too, Henryk continued to reminisce, closing his eyes.

Miron wiped his mouth on his sleeve and said:

At that post of yours, did you ever mess around with a negress?

He laughed hoarsely, scratching his temple with a claw-like finger.

A boor. You're just a boor. You're a degenerate. A retired degenerate, said Henryk. Spitting copiously as he did so.

He had something else to say. He opened his mouth. He stretched his neck. He looked as if he were daydreaming. But his reverie was the result of brief cerebral ischemia.

Eat. Eat up, so your stomachs won't rumble—it's so unattractive, warned Benia.

I didn't tell you, but apparently another person passed away in the night.

Leon took off his glasses. He squinted. He looked toward the entrance gate and said:

Napoleon wasn't the victim of arsenic poisoning. He died of a tumor. I say, he died of a tumor. I often think about him. It's odd, very odd. As a historical figure—

He suddenly broke off. He wanted to say something else, but he couldn't remember what.

That's just talk. He croaked of cancer? Napoleon? A fine historian you are, huffed Miron, slobbering on his shirt.

It was the defeat. The French national disaster. A man who's failed dies. And that's that. He knows he lost, he goes to bed, lies down, and never gets up again. The life pours out of him. Like milk boiling over in a pot. That's what.

He was tired out. His breathing was slow.

Yes, dear Miron is right. A person soon clears off when there's no cash to pay for treatment, agreed Benia.

That Napoleon couldn't have died of cancer, no way. My brother had cancer. He worked at the depot. He got kidney cancer. A common death. For common people. But even so he had it good. He didn't want to be old. And that's why he died early. Fifty-three years of age. In July. July sixteenth he died. In the afternoon. And on the twenty-first he was buried. Summer.

Helena moved on her chair.

What can you do? It's hot. The body ferments if you like it or not.

Eat. Eat up, advised Benia.

When my wife's little Minxy died, first of all she trembled. Then she went under the radiator. She just about squeezed in between the ribs, recalled Leon.

Miron rapped his fingers against the table top.

Yes, dogs tremble for a long time first, and then wham-bam, they give up the ghost. And they're stiff already. Done for already. My neighbor had a bitch, a German shepherd. But they'd cut off her tail. Like they do to boxers.

Our little Minxy.

Leon's eyes glazed over.

Sometimes I can see her looking at me with those sweet little eyes of hers. Or being overjoyed when I walk in the door. She jumps up on the armchair, or the couch. What is there to say.

He broke off, weeping.

Bing bang bong, I'm dead and gone, said Miron, cheering up.

He wiped his face with his shirt front. His bloodshot eyeballs looked as if they'd been forcibly pressed into too small sockets.

For a while they ate in silence. As at neighboring tables.

Helena gazed straight ahead. Toward the gate.

Henryk was tired out from raising his spoon. He leaned backward and sniffed the air.

The sea, the sea. I can smell the sea. It must be very close. And gulls. The atmosphere is soaked in fish oil today. I can smell it.

Why do you go on about the sea? said Miron irritably.

The sea and then the sea again. On and on about the sea. We're in the capital city. Our country's capital city.

Henryk didn't answer.

He was staring at the man at the next table. He was drinking from a children's mug, his dry lips could barely grab hold of the spout protruding from the closed lid.

The staff were ever wearier, their charges seemed immune to the heat wave.

For the residents, as at any other season, the time was spent on vying over their foreign illnesses, spying, stalking, telling tales, and teasing those condemned to a wheelchair. The more able-bodied purloined correspondence, and appropriated other people's wedding photos and pictures of their children.

Worst of all was visiting day. The waiting for loved ones generally proved in vain, and consequently degenerated into sneering at each other's wigs, snatching walking frames, pulling hair, tearing off toupees, hiding crutches, boasting of their educated children, driving the childless to tears, spitting in the faces of the staff, and peeing on hands while diapers were changed.

Everyone had fears about their health. In fact, they'd have preferred to make do without bodies. Each of the residents wanted to have a unique, refined ailment. They were all afraid of brown gums, and none of the men wanted to have prostate trouble.

Prostate. The gland that expands, as the manager said of it. You might be too late for the toilet, piss on your slippers or pants, and letting go in your shorts was definitely impossible to hide. Only last week two of the gentlemen were transferred to the house by the lake for this very reason. The manager would pick out the sick at mealtimes. He'd cruise the tables, until at last, with a broad smile on his face, he'd stop before one of the delinquents.

So what did I hear from the doctor today? he'd start off cryptically.

You've finally grown a prostate gland. All because the esteemed gentleman hasn't copulated for at least twenty years. Huh? Or perhaps I'm wrong, and one of the old biddies here present has given you a loan of her muffin? Well, what's the truth? We'll soon find out. Sexual abstinence, or has Barbie been flapping her veiny old legs in the air?

Brown gums were also a constant source of worry. The residents knew they should air their dentures on the windowsill, and rinse their mouths frequently. And at great length. Best of all with water containing citric acid slipped them by the well-paid cook.

After all, bad breath could be a reason for transfer to the house by the lake. The manager was very sensitive to it:

Szymon, your kisser stinks like an old bloodhound's.

Miron, do me a favor, don't say good day to me, because it's puke-making. Like walking past a slaughterhouse full of flyblown carcasses.

Leokadia, perhaps it's time for a nice little room with a view of the lake, huh? Those gums of yours can barely hold onto your dentures.

The manager stopped talking. He was about to address Henryk, but suddenly scowled on seeing Leon giving him the finger like a schoolboy.

Mr. Rabinowicz, how can I give you a positive response? he asked in a weary, irritated tone.

I repeat: the health department will not give its consent. Mr. Rabinowicz, we don't need a mongrel here too. You were an engineer, weren't you? If you'd been an animal breeder, perhaps I could manage to understand your pathetic attempt to simulate your old life, but—

He broke off. Leon got up and stood straight as a ramrod.

Please don't reduce my request to the level of a compensatory fantasy. I specialized in chaos theory.

Leon's glasses were askew. He continued to stand straight. He rubbed his marmalade-stained shirt.

The manager grew impatient. He was sweating profusely. He

wiped his brow with the back of his hand. He spoke rapidly, in a raised tone:

I am a physicist. I am a physicist. You were a physicist, Mr. Rabinowicz. Yes, and you're applying to me to keep a dog. Oy, shame on us, shame on us. Chaos theory. That's a good one. There'd be chaos all right if I were to pander to the whims of every resident here. This guy wants a dog, that guy wants a high-class hooker in black stockings with tits like melons, this dame wants an emasculated macho to read her psalms at bedtime. And that one wants references addressed to the dear Lord to get her into heaven.

The manager paused, wiped the sweat from his shining nose, and said:

I'd like to introduce our new recruit.

Who's that? asked Henryk, resting his head on the back of his deck chair. And fell asleep without waiting for an answer.

Here's the new volunteer. She's going to take care of the residents' feet.

There are still some good people left in the world. She won't stand it here for long, whispered Leokadia.

She got up from the table. For several days she hadn't been able to eat. She was deluding herself that the reason for this was the heat. But in fact she knew it was because of the creepy-crawlies. Everywhere she could see tormented, multi-legged insects. In the bread basket, speeding down the passages, lurking in slippers, in inadequately rinsed-out chamber pots, or drowned in breakfast bowls full of milk soup. Roaches crawling along the edges of dozing residents' half-open mouths.

Leokadia wanted to dispel her negative thoughts. She trudged toward the volunteer to sign up for a treatment as fast as possible.

Leokadia's feet. Swollen. Blue. Puffy from the heat. Her toes were crooked, and the big ones made it hard to walk. She was determined to improve her circulation. She wanted to lie down in her room with her feet on a pillow. If she could manage to raise them that high.

As she was passing the new volunteer, she forgot what she wanted to ask her about. With a set face and half-closed eyes she kept moving forward. She stopped briefly in the passage. She noticed some languid green flies, stock-still on the paneling. Someone had smeared butter on it, which was going rancid in the warmth.

She plodded on. Then she rested again. By the treatment room. After a few minutes her body stopped reacting to the omnipresent human stench, mixed with the smell of Lysol, chlorine, and starch.

For Helena things were different. She had never gotten used to it. She vomited on the instant. The smell of chlorine. That same odor. Chlorine had been sprayed in the freight cars that took them to the camp.

Has the mailman arrived?

She heard a voice coming from the nearest room.

She turned her head. The door was open. On the floor amid some toy railcars sat Wiktor.

Yes, Wiktor? Can I fetch you something? Summon somebody, perhaps?

Was there something for me? From my son?

A whistling breath announced an interval between one word and the next.

Wiktor, give me a break. For four years there's been nothing for you. There's nobody to write to you. Your son drowned in some fancy country. Was it Greece?

Oh, yes, there was something of the kind.

He whistled.

You don't weep for him anymore.

Leokadia's voice cracked, like that of a boy going through puberty.

So what do you know about despair, huh? Gonna give me lessons, are you? Our teacher-lady of seven sorrows has been found, he muttered.

Leokadia nodded.

You're playing with toy trains. If I were to start dressing up a dolly, I'd be regarded as a senile old coot. But you're allowed.

He wasn't listening.

He set the electric railroad in motion.

The railcars moved off, vanished behind an armchair, fleetingly appeared beneath the table, flashed under the bed, dodged the chamber pot and the warped knee boots in a graceful arc, and once again raced past Wiktor. They hid behind the armchair. Then appeared beneath the table.

Leokadia shuffled on. She stopped to steady her breathing. She leaned against a windowsill.

She saw Helena and that new resident, Bożydar, standing at the bottom of the garden. They must have hidden in the rose bushes to avoid the caregivers. They had little sticks in their mouths, they were smoking, the scallywags.

Bożydar seemed satisfied. As the new arrivals usually did, not yet having forgotten their old, minor habits. But it would happen very quickly.

Helena shouldn't smoke. Leokadia promised herself she'd tell the caregiver on duty that those two were smoking in the bushes. Her only fear was that she might forget about it. She must get to her room as fast as possible and make a note of it.

Suddenly she remembered the manager's remark about her gums. Maybe there weren't any roaches at that house by the lake? she wondered. Somebody had said conditions there must be better if the sickest and most dependent residents were moved there.

Once again, afternoon tea trickled on until supper.

This was when the third daily dose of drugs was distributed. Hot water with sugar was poured into plastic cups, while bread and butter, processed cheese, and tasteless pâtés were set out on the tables.

Benia prayed before the meal:

The Lord is my shepherd. I shall not want. You lead me beside still waters, You guide me along straight paths. Your goodness and mercy shall follow me all the days of my life.

Some of the residents were wrapped in woolen blankets. Those being fed stared into space. Peaceful. Forsaken. They did more sleeping than eating. Others, more independent, lapped up their vegetable purée and, as every day, complained about its bland flavor, in need of salt.

I can smell the sea, I swear it. The open sea, a light breeze. The rippling azure, declared Henryk, as if trying to convince them all.

The sea. Can't you smell it? The sea. I taught my own daughter to swim. She was ten when we started swimming far out into the Baltic. We swam very close together. Side by side. On the return journey she'd climb onto my back. I swam slowly. So she could catch her breath. We liked it best on the days when there were hardly any waves.

He gasped, weary. Sweaty.

What a strange tale, wheezed Miron.

Our dear old Consul is a regular sea wolf. All our widows will have someone to sigh for tonight. Let's get to work, ladies. Better to sigh than to die, huh? he said, and rapped against the table top.

Helena was gazing in the direction of the entrance gate. Once again it was clearly visible.

Darkness was falling, the sun was patiently giving way to the shadows of two large hornbeams. Their dark trunks were gleaming, perhaps because of the very recent rain. Everything was cooling off. Imperceptibly, so it seemed.

Do not leave me, Savior, restrain Your fierce wrath. In the name of the Father and the Son, and the Holy Ghost. Amen. Eat. Eat up. To be well ahead, urged Benia.

Someone passed on. In the night, muttered Leon, scratching his unevenly shaved cheeks.

Did you folks hear? Shouts, scurrying. All of a sudden. Too quickly to call the doctor. I went into the corridor. They chased me away. It was well past midnight. Did you hear, my dears? Do you know who's missing? I can't do the reckoning. It all happened so quickly.

So the whole summer's going to be this muggy, is it? said Benia gladly.

Now they'll run movies about penguins more often. As soon as I see snow on TV I feel cold. I don't even have to eat ice cream, she added.

Helena turned toward her and said:

Yes, Benia. Yes. It's already summer. Summer again. Leolka, you probably want to be able to watch the sheep again. Sated and idle, lolling on the hillsides. Clover grass is such a dark green.

She looked at her sister.

She wanted to add more, about the moist meadows where warm rain sprinkles the clover and the sheep laze around, snuggling up to each other. But now she just gazed in silence at Leokadia, who was using her index finger to pick food off her dentures.

The sisters had arrived together. As they wished, they had been given separate rooms, but for meals they were assigned a small table for two. They were not pleased about it.

Helena would have preferred to eat in wider company, and Leokadia's desire was not to be supervised. She was bad at hiding her loathing of everything that was meant to pass her gullet. She didn't like putting anything into her body. She couldn't bear the thought of anything from the outside ending up on the inside, within her body.

It made her happy to hide a piece of cake dripping with juice in her pocket. A bit of bread roll or a slice of yellow cheese, tucked under her cuff like a handkerchief.

Helena had had them moved to a larger table. In company the chances of hiding something were even smaller.

Helena strenuously leaned forward. She extracted a sugar lump from the bowl. Like the Host, she placed it on her tongue. Bored. Sleepy. She winced. On the steps she saw a resident in his pajama top and a rather yellow pair of long johns, baggy at the knees. He was struggling, trying to loosen the elastic holding them up.

He shouted:

Wretches. Not a squeak. Wretches. They never learn a thing. Nothing. They just whisper in corners. But I have an occupational disease. A raw throat. Calluses on the vocal cords. Three rest cures didn't help. No sanatorium can do a thing. But they've become so talkative. On and on, droning away. They're not even bothered by my deafness. But not a squeak before the blackboard. Morons. Dunces.

Gasping, he sank to the grass. Down on all fours, like a blind man who has lost something, he felt the ground with the flat of his hands. While smiling. And nodding.

Leokadia was watching him too. At first she seemed sad, but after a while she looked at her sister and said in a shrill, joyful tone:

Apparently there are places on Earth with thirty-eight varieties of wild orchid and nineteen species of bee. Isn't that marvelous, Helena?

Bing bang bong, I'm dead and gone, interposed Miron.

Leokadia smiled at her sister:

Just imagine lying down amid all that greenery, listening to the insects buzzing and nothing else, just lying there. Are you listening to me? she asked.

Helena smiled by way of affirmation, but her eyes remained narrowed, as if absent. Briefly they sought something in her sister's face, then, suddenly startled, they withdrew to her plate.

Are you listening? pressed Leokadia.

Yes, yes. I'm listening, I am, she replied mechanically. Almost angrily.

But that fellow over there annoys me. Do you see? He's sniffing the grass, any moment now he'll be eating it. And I have to spend my time with people like that. Just think whom I used to dine with.

Leokadia took advantage of her sister's agitation to roll some vegetable matter into a little ball, drain off the liquid, and tuck it into the puffed sleeve of her silk blouse.

She began to explain patiently:

He was a math teacher. That's why the sight of him upsets people. He never stops radiating integrals, logarithms, and compound fractions. There's no need to be so angry with the residents.

Helena interrupted her:

You know, you and that fellow, you two have something in common.

For goodness' sake, Helena, you're annoyed with me again.

Don't you want to know what unites you?

True love to your dying day, interposed Miron, wincing at the pain in his groin.

No. Please, I beg you, whispered Leokadia.

She'd rather talk about flowers and ladybugs. But her sister was upset about something. Her neck was covered in red streaks. Any moment now she'd berate her in a raised tone. Maybe even search her pockets and cuffs. Extract the food and tell her to eat it. Not let her leave the table until she'd swallowed it all.

Helena grabbed her by the hand:

You both shuffle your feet in the same odious way, you see. How many times have I told you: Raise your knees higher, Leokadia. You walk like a hideous old woman. I cannot look at you. This morning, when you came onto the terrace, I was so ashamed I thought the earth would swallow me up.

Don't be angry, don't be angry. I won't do it anymore. You're out of sorts today, Helena.

Leokadia glanced at her sister. Helena was calming down. She stared vacantly at the sugar bowl.

It's because of the heat, she said.

Do you know what our Consul Henryk said about me? said Leokadia, in an effort to cheer her up. To distract her, so she'd forget about the search, and not try to find her hiding places for food.

Helena grabbed her by the hand.

Can't you guess what he said. Fortune has granted Leokadia the greatest gift. After all she has been through, she's still able to be as happy as a sheep's tail.

Yes, that's exactly what I said. In those very words, agreed Henryk, sitting up straight in his chair.

I've said it many a time. But my comment about you, dear Helena, was that you're the proudest of the women here. Please forgive me, you other ladies. Dear Helena, don't keep running away from us. Is that a nice thing to do? A mature woman behaving like a teenager. Zip, without a word, off she runs. Leaving us here, disconsolate.

He broke off, and glanced at the target of his request.

Without a word, Helena put another sugar lump on her tongue. She stared into space.

Helena's reverie allowed Leokadia to get away with stuffing some bread under her stockings, into her slippers, behind her waist band, and into the warm spot between her blouse and her undershirt.

At the house that Leokadia had vacated she had left plenty of food behind, stuffed into corners. In the electricity meter closet, behind the picture of some roe deer, in the box for sewing thread, in the old, unused washing machine, in cracks in the floor. Decayed, damp, moldy. Stuck fast. Kept safe. A chronicle of past hunger.

Don't eat so many sweets. Sugar excites you, Helena. And if you over-sweeten your bowels, that's a guaranteed upset, and diarrhea in heat like this, she rebuked her sister.

She could feel an unpleasant burden in her belly. As if her guts were toppling onto their left-hand side. Trying to devour themselves. She pursed her lips. She suppressed her nausea.

Helena slowly swallowed the sugar that had dissolved in her mouth.

In a tone devoid of emotion, she said:

Apparently it's going to be a very fine summer. But that's no reason to be so gleeful. Especially like a sheep's tail.

She shielded her mouth with her hand. She wanted to shout. She had a sudden urge to shout. To shout enough to make herself fall over. Make them finally carry her off to the house by the lake. And allow Leolka not to have to swallow anything.

Helena took ages to calm down. She gazed at the flowers in their pots, at the dusted leathery leaves of the rubber plants. At last her gaze landed on Truda. She was sitting in a wheelchair, clutching her purse tightly to her chest. The skin of her face was like the skin that covers the scrotum. Her mouth looked as if it were glued shut. Garishly red with crookedly applied lipstick. The hand that had put it on must have been shaking. Not so long ago Helena had spent most of her time with Truda. She was so good at telling stories. She'd had an interesting life. She had set up libraries in villages. She had traveled a lot. She'd known so many writers. Once a year her four daughters and eight grandchildren came to visit her. On these occasions, she'd always summon Helena. She'd praise her beauty and elegance, and introduce her as her confidante and best friend.

Since Easter Truda had hardly spoken a word. Sometimes she just stared at Helena, trying to remember where she knew her from. But she couldn't fish anything out of her memory, not a scrap of conversation. Nothing that would allow her to domesticate Helena. Stop treating her as a stranger. It never worked. For

Truda the present world was gone. But just to make sure, right at the end, just as she was about to leave, with one hand clutching her purse, she raised the other, wagged a threatening finger and commanded Helena: You must pack, dear lady. The Germans are coming. The Germans are coming now. You must pack.

Day after day, the sun sizzled in the empty sky.

Every time he visited, the priest repeated that the summer would be long and bountiful.

At daybreak, before breakfast, clouds appeared that looked like tufts of cotton candy. Szymon watched as the sun slowly melted them. Despite the season, he always wore the same felt overcoat. It was a gift from Momma twenty years ago on the day he was promoted to chief accountant. Each morning he trailed around the garden, then he spent the whole day sitting in the common room. It's cooler and the birds don't chirp as much, he explained to the nurse.

He didn't like company. Stimulating pastimes, cutting out, coloring in, catching a ball thrown by a caregiver.

He wanted to be alone. All his life he'd run away from people. But they were constantly coming to him for something. They knew he could help them to sort out a thing or two. So they kept knocking at his door. Cheated on their expenses. Pretended they'd lost the receipts, fibbed, inflated the invoices, argued over their daily allowance, lied, and tried to include things that didn't count. And a year before his retirement the board had tried to persuade him to do some creative bookkeeping. He hadn't yielded.

All his life he had lived with his mother. A taciturn seamstress. A valued employee of the Żoliborzanka tailoring firm. She in one room, Szymon in the other with his goldfish, Cutie.

In the evenings his mother received her clients. Fat, shameless women. They'd undress with the door half open. They'd stick out their tushes, pull in their tummies, and scratch at their thighs. They'd laugh out loud, and shift from foot to foot, as the tailor's tape measure slid across their bodies like a lover's sweaty paw.

The apartment was steeped in their sweat, the odor of the chamomile lotion they rubbed into their hair, and their cheap perfume bought at the street market in little bottles with numbered labels.

Szymon would peep at them through the gap in the door as they twisted in all directions. They'd dally over the choice of cut. They'd fuss, grow impatient, fret and fume at themselves, with a frill or without, perhaps a yoke or a boat neck? The bodies brimmed over, there were lengths of material spilled around the room, scattered trimmings, pins trapped by a small magnet and clumped together, old jam jars full of buttons, half-closed drawers containing spools, rolls of packing paper, and greasy pages from old journals.

When they departed, humming to themselves on the stairs, they left behind a smell of sweaty groin, and the gurgle of a malevolent underbelly that lured and repelled, tempted and repulsed. The rattle of the sewing machine would slow down Szymon's breathing. Soothe his trembling hands, the part-dreams, part-fantasies or horrible images that were swilling around in his mind, in which he'd stop being chief accountant and become a tailor with nimble fingers able to determine the client's dimensions by touch, to the last quarter inch. He could see himself kneeling at the feet of glamorous women. He'd take the measurement, laying his hands on bare flesh. He'd finger. Gather skin by the handful. As if ruffling material. Mumble with a mouthful of pins. As if by accident rest his head against a slightly bulging belly, as hard as the base of a tin bowl. He'd look at the client from below, at the barely visible head, obscured by the prominent breasts caught in a harness: whalebone, buckles, hooks and eyes. He'd feel as if a splendid mare were appearing before his face, rather than a woman. A skittish creature that bowed to his touch, not just some guy's wife. At these moments Szymon was filled with satisfaction. It suffused his body.

First Momma passed on, then Cutie. He was floating inertly. Head down. A thread of feces trailed behind him.

Szymon buried Cutie by his momma's grave. The fish fit in a cigarette packet lined with absorbent cotton. On the little mound of earth he placed a shell brought home from a seaside vacation. At the time, he and Momma had bought themselves sailor caps. Because of a kidney condition Momma drank a lot of beer at a booth on the pier and laughed out loud. Like never before. Maybe this surfeit of joy, the outburst of something that should have been hidden, firmly locked deep in the soul, maybe that was the reason why, for ages after their return from the seaside, whenever a client visited, Momma was sad about something.

Szymon was sure he'd go the same way as Momma. He'd hit his head on the door frame. He'd fall. Blood would flow from his nose. But he went on and on living.

The neighbors reported him for failing to switch off the gas. Water would pour into the tub for days on end, and the radio set to full volume wouldn't let them sleep. The management of the housing cooperative decided that Szymon had become a danger. But he was sure he had fallen victim to vengeful tenants. He spat at the children when they gawped at him in the elevator. He refused to throw out some sacks of rotten potatoes stored in the cellar. They started taking pictures of him relieving himself in the garbage chute.

The day before his departure he overdosed on purgatives. He managed to relieve himself on all the tenants' doormats.

In summer the residents spent most of the day on the terrace. Only Szymon sat in the common room. Once the tables were removed it became large, and every word bounced off the bare walls marked by damp patches from last year's plumbing disaster, every whisper grew to a roar.

Occasionally Bożydar, the still-new arrival, came in here. Large, burly, always in a red cap and combat shorts. The twisted, bulging varicose veins on his calves matched his blue sneakers.

He sat pensively writing something down in a notebook, turning and rustling the pages.

It's hard to find a real momma for children now, said Szymon.

He felt obliged to tell every newbie something about his life.

You're sure to be disgusted by the world of women too.

He broke off to take a close look at the white, curly hairs on his interlocutor's chest, on which hung a gold chain burdened with a cross.

There's even scientific proof that women think about things they shouldn't every three seconds, he added.

I should hope so, said Bożydar, without looking up from his notebook.

They all go crazy for me. But what matters to me personally is quality, not quantity.

He nodded over his notebook.

But they don't think about what's good for the family, stated Szymon.

Just, you know what.

He paused meaningfully.

Horrible, truly. Even on public transport. Their smell. You've noticed it, huh? As if they've just been doing it. They go on about their feelings all the time, but they actually feel so little. They feel so little. Did you hear what I said? he asked insistently.

French women are real stunners, said Bożydar, smacking his lips.

I went on a trip to France. That's quite a tower they've put up for themselves. You should be sorry you never saw it. Three days in Paris. Real stunners. Mouth-watering. Just the sight of them.

He whistled, spitting on his notebook.

Szymon leaned toward Bożydar.

Women have no respect for a decent man, they don't. All of them, to the very last, prefer shady types. Despicable slimeballs. They want to be humiliated. Beaten. Knocked around. Dragged into the bushes. Told lies. Told barefaced lies. Abandoned. And then begged for forgiveness. On your knees. Barefoot. In nothing but your socks. But when they come across a civilized guy. Placid. A homebody. They despise that. It means nothing to them, huh? Do you agree?

Szymon was trying in vain to catch his interlocutor's eye.

Bożydar tore his gaze from his notebook, and rearranged the lie of his testicles in his shorts.

The heat. It's hard to sleep. Will you sign my petition? To stop them from shutting off the television after ten.

I'm a chief accountant. You can see for yourself that I can't put my name to any old thing, said Szymon. And continued:

There was even a time when I wanted to have a go at being a father, but what can you do? You know, that's why I gave up on love. To them we're just working capital.

He sighed.

Ten people have already signed, counted Bożydar aloud, and made a note in a corner of the page.

My priority was to keep things in order. Especially once Momma was lying down almost all the time. Dust wiped. Pots scrubbed. Floors too. Handkerchiefs starched.

Szymon broke off. He winced. He scratched his cheek. His fingers were like skewers. Gone yellow.

Into the dining room came Helena. With an inhalator pressed to her mouth. He didn't like her. She smoked in the rose bushes. She smelled of cigarettes. Szymon hoped they'd catch her smoking soon, and cart her off to the house by the lake.

Once he'd been witness to an attack of breathlessness she'd had in the treatment room. Her hat had fallen off, and he'd seen her skull covered in clumps of hair, the damp skin shining from under it, as if soaking wet.

He sighed, and stuck out his tongue at Helena behind her back. He stood up. And trudged off to look for another refuge.

He stopped on the threshold, remembering the bioenergetic therapist's instructions, raised his hands and wound his fingers around his neck. He stood like that for a long while, waiting for a surge of vital energy from the cosmos. With his eyes half-closed and his head slightly raised. His distended Adam's apple, dark blue and purple, slid from top to bottom in his dry, stringy neck. He sighed. Several times. Unexpectedly loud.

Helena was relaxing her breathing following her walk. She stood in the middle of the common room like a hungry she-cat, staring at Szymon's Adam's apple.

He finally lowered his hands, and without looking at her left the room.

Helena sat down on his chair. She felt quite all right, her bones didn't ache like yesterday. She was certain the summer was good for her.

Tomorrow I'll have cigarettes, she said.

Bożydar raised his head.

She tossed the inhalator into a little red bag, adjusted her skirt, and looked him straight in the eyes.

No kidding, where from? wondered Bożydar.

Her porcelain teeth lit up her suntanned face.

The priest will bring them for me. He's a good man.

Will you treat me to one?

Of course. But this time you'll have to smoke quickly. They'll finish sunbathing and come after us.

Right. All that time sunning themselves on the terrace has made our little nurses look like half-breeds. Will you sign? My petition. For the television.

I'm second on the list. I gave you my autograph yesterday in the dining room. But I can sign for my sister. How I loved my television set. I found this channel. Well after midnight, when there was nothing else on, they showed a fireplace. Filling the whole screen. All night long. Isn't that marvelous? warbled Helena.

A TV set by day, a fireplace by night. I bought my first TV with money from the Germans. For the camp. It was called a Belvedere. I loved it like a child. There was enough left to buy a Victory watch for nine hundred zlotys, but I don't wear it. It's too heavy. And my wine-red pantsuit. With my figure I looked very chic. It went well with a cape made of crease-resistant worsted. Each night I'd sit in my armchair. Close, very close, and I'd watch. It didn't matter what they broadcast. It was the humming. I even liked to leave it on while I was cleaning. I just wanted it to be running. As if the house were full of people.

She paused for a moment.

Now I never watch it at all. I hate the television room. I hate those old coots. They use mothballs for talc. The whole company's as deaf as a post. The television roars away at full blast. But watching TV is an intimate sort of experience, don't you think?

I agree with you entirely, said Bożydar.

The agony of holding back the urge to scratch his itchy groin was visible on his face.

I have applied for a television set. An individual one. Just for my room. When do you think they'll look into it? she asked.

As soon as you kick the bucket. Then they'll look into it, as if they're so good and kind. What's your first name? I keep forgetting to ask.

Helena.

That's nice. Ah, what a pretty name. Lovely, lovely. And mine is Bożydar—God's gift.

Bożydar. Wonderful. Promising. Sometimes I don't think I can stand being here among all these old coots any longer. Museum pieces, not men. Empty shells. Do you feel the same way about being here in general?

I haven't had time to get tired of it yet. It's great. Summertime. The terrace. The garden. You can have a chat. Run a campaign. I was president of an angling club, and at my housing development I established three community parking lots.

What on earth are you saying? said Helena indignantly.

I hate this place. I can't sleep properly here. All these years. Nothing but sleepless nights since I first arrived. In the past, as soon as I put my head to the pillow I was off. It's all because of the mattress. As hard as stone. Like in the army. But I can still tell the difference between a better or worse bed. I've spent a long time lying on a stretcher before now. And that's quite enough. I've heard that if you have bedsores they're very good for the spine. But they only have them in the room for the centenarians. Oh, how I hate this place. As for those eggs in ersatz horseradish sauce yesterday, did you eat them? They sit in the stomach, don't they? The dinners here are so sad. I miss the city. The stores. The cafés. I adore the scent of freshly roasted coffee. I'd go to the university too. I liked to sit on a bench there. Watch the young people. But what is there here? That's why I've run away twice. But third time lucky. I won't give in so easily.

I did a good turn, said Bożydar.

My grandson got married. They had no place to live. I gave them my room. So far I'm not complaining. As long as the people are willing to sign petitions everything will be all right.

The people? she said, snorting.

When I came to live here, I discovered to my horror that I look far better than the entire staff. I am made for social life, not herd life. But what do we have for entertainment here? Games of Ring Around the Rosie. Old Maid. Baa Baa Black Sheep. Simon Says.

Simon says, where did you leave your dentures? added Bożydar.

Helena's blood-red painted lips cracked into a broad smile, showing her pearly-white teeth and blue gums covered in white flecks.

Are you a widower? she asked, smoothing the fabric on her hip.

Twice over. But to be strictly honest, I was only with the first one for a year. She was too jealous. And a jealous woman is worse than a house fire.

He laughed, noticing Helena's shoes. They were black pumps, and the lacquer was sprinkled with golden glitter. He couldn't tear his eyes away. Ah, so he wasn't doomed to the sight of nothing but worn-out slippers, stiff bootees, and clogs.

I noticed you at once. You're not incontinent yet. And you don't dribble, he said admiringly.

I am a widow. But I don't neglect myself, like the other female residents, she replied, without looking at him.

I love to take care of myself, and no one can stop me. Even the pressure to cut my hair. To them I look like a witch. They're afraid of me. They're afraid of me in these beautiful curls. But I want to woman up. I want to, you see.

She laughed.

I won't let them treat me like an old crone. Why should I regard myself the way others regard me. Maybe I should be encouraging the women here to sit plucking feathers? Or to spin, perhaps? They can't do a thing to me. They think they can mock me? I'm not afraid. I'm still proud of my appearance. I'm not crumpled, am I?

What do you mean? Everyone knows you're the epitome of elegance.

As long as I look nice, it means I'm still alive. I knew that as a child.

She shrugged.

You know what, I was always very pretty. I had lice, scabies, scarlet fever, and typhus, but I also had my looks. Like a cover girl. Dr. Josef was able to appreciate that. Whenever a commission came to the camp, they immediately put me on display. You don't know who's sitting here before you, do you? Well, you'll never guess. No one ever does.

Helena paused for a moment, took a deep breath and said:

Here before you, my dear friend, is Miss Auschwitz. Yes, it's true. Miss Auschwitz.

What did you— Yes. But . . . Yes?

Miss Auschwitz. The former little Miss Auschwitz. How beautiful I was. When I arrived at the camp, I had such sweet little arms. They tattooed me on the thigh.

She nodded, and adjusted her skirt.

She stared at the tip of her shoe.

They didn't cut my hair. Dr. Josef liked to look at it.

I had a more normal sort of life, said Bożydar.

Except that my mother died suddenly. When the news broke that there was freedom, we all raced outside. People ran ahead, hugging each other and shouting. That guy in the airplane was pleased too. He flew low, raking the ground, and blasted away at everything moving in front of him. Including Momma.

He was lost for words.

Helena helped him:

Momma stopped moving too? Is that what you mean?

Well, yes. I ran up. She was lying on her front, with her arms and legs spreadeagled. As if biting the earth. I couldn't see her face. Someone was shouting. All around there was glass from the windows, slashed walls, branches torn off by shells everywhere. I reached her. I pressed against her. Tightly. So tight it hurt. Stupid, huh? I threw her arm around my shoulders. And stayed like that all night. Cuddled up to her. I cried. I lost my voice. And I'm still hoarse to this day. That's what happened. It's not something to talk about. It was only next day that they found us. They were robbing corpses, you know, gold and all that. I was very young. Four or five years old.

What was your mom's hair like? asked Helena.

She couldn't tear her gaze from the bruises she had just discovered on Bożydar's calves: large veins, twisted into bulging knots.

Fair. Blonde. And she had these little curls. Here, above the brow.

Bożydar pointed.

She liked doing her hair. Getting dressed up. That's what they said about her. When I asked questions later on. I was grown up by then. My father was killed in the war. I tried looking for family members. But there was no one.

What about her face? What was it like? she went on questioning him.

Pretty. Oval. But at that time, after the war, everyone was thin as a rake. She was a good singer. As a child she sang in the church choir. Her voice was high-pitched, enough to make your heart ache. I remember that. She had me very late. She prayed, she'd lost all hope, and then I came along. That's why she christened me Bożydar—God's gift.

You know what, I can't remember my mom. Is that normal? said Helena.

I was almost twelve when we were separated. But not to remember anything at all? Strange, it's so strange. I don't even know what I looked like as a child. After the war, at the orphanage, they didn't take pictures. But I mean the ones from the camp. They took lots of photographs of me. On the stretcher. On the dissecting table. With Dr. Josef, putting his arm around my waist. He could fully embrace me with one arm. I was a puny little thing. That white glove of his. It looked like a belt. He showed me the picture. He leaned over the stretcher and showed me. I could smell his cologne. He smiled and asked: Did I know my daddy was dead? He took a great interest in me, you know. He'd even told his assistant to find out in the barrack why Daddy wasn't waving to me anymore. That cologne of his. I can smell it to this day. He told me himself that my dad had had to go into the oven.

You've had a tough life. But there's no sign of it on you, concluded Bożydar.

The manager and the staff praise me for it. When a journalist came, and wrote an article about homes like this one, they sent me. Because I looked so nice. Altogether still quite good-looking. Well-groomed. Fragrant. Talkative. With no memory gaps. And no diapers. I can be touched without gloves or disgust. They could lend me to the house by the lake as a living advertisement.

I'm not surprised. Personally I'm not surprised. You don't look as if you went through the camp, said Bożydar, nodding.

I had TB, scurvy, listed Helena, scabies, frostbitten toes. But in spite of that I looked well. There was something in me that meant I flourished there. Like a flower in the desert. A lovely little flower.

Tired, she fell silent.

Bożydar only spoke after a long pause:

As I stressed earlier. Generally speaking, I like you. Why not? It's a shame for you to lead a solitary life. There are plenty of eligible jackets and ties in the world. Even here. You could still get something going.

Helena watched indifferently as Bożydar bashfully tugged at a corner of a page.

Do I understand your meaning correctly, dear Bożydar? I'm not quite sure, how could I settle down with someone from here? Please don't think me heartless. But all these men. If they're not deaf, they have a prostate. A Zimmer frame, a walker. Or they dribble so dreadfully that their chins are wet. Or they can't control their bowels. Or they spend all day long crumbling bread for the pigeons. And one of the centenarians from the second floor mistakes me for his mother. It's a nightmare. Perhaps you can tell from my appearance that the candidates for my hand all had higher qualifications. Members of the bar, I tell you. Two attorneys. An orthopedist with extensive doctoral diplomas. A retired Chief Justice. Good old Anatol. I don't even know where his children took him off to. They were afraid I'd inherit his property. Two attorneys. And they were all widowers. Not divorced men with hidden flaws. Or old bachelors with their own nasty habits. No, they were very decent men. I can assure you.

I don't have to sweet-talk you. You know for yourself that in your category you're a Barbie, said Bożydar.

A brief silence set in.

What am I waiting for here? Helena asked herself, adjusting her blouse.

Why am I suffering away here with this company? With all these old coots. And to think that some of them want to vegetate here for another ten years. Live to a hundred. Get their certificate from the manager. Be interviewed for the local television. Be given a cake by the nurses that the nurses will eat themselves later on. Because with our livers, gallbladders and stomachs, none of us can even touch such a big dose of compound sugars, she said, laughing.

My heart has no one to beat for anymore, declared Bożydar, closing his notebook.

But it's beating. The old pump is still thumping away. What can you do. Everyone wants to live a long time. Even us folks here. We want to live.

She interrupted him:

It's pitiful. Listen up. Two hundred years ago, when a person got past forty, they knew they didn't have much time left. But what about now? We demand attention, care, and we have nothing to give in return but tales of what tormented us. Or what entertained us. But what tormented us is of no concern to anyone anymore. And they don't find the things that entertained us the least bit amusing. I can understand the desire to prolong something that gives us pleasure. But why want old age to last longer and longer? To put all our suffering, pain, defects, and mourning in formaldehyde? If I live to two hundred, I won't be any happier.

Helena clenched her lips.

That's why we find small pleasures, suggested Bożydar, amused by her rebellion. She was so alive when she was sulky.

Tiny pleasures. Looking through photos. Soaking your dentures, said Helena.

Remembering the deceased. Parading around in our diapers. Showing our you-know-what. Grumbling about our children's ingratitude. Summoning up non-requited loves. Everything. Anything at all.

She suddenly stopped talking.

Admiring our friends' wonderful curls. What fabulous hair you have. It's amber, not hair, enthused Bożydar.

What wonderful hair I used to have. Down to my knees. Like a cape. A little coat of hair, said Helena, adjusting the leg of her pantsuit.

You have to be well-groomed, then everyone knows you're healthy. I was quite a doll, that's why I survived. But. After the war things got worse and worse. Momma. I don't remember her. Not her face, or her eyes, nothing. Only that she put a little comb into my pocket. They let me keep it on the loading ramp. Maybe because it was nothing special. Cheap. Brown. Missing a few teeth. I always clutched it in my fist as I slept. At the camp, at the orphanage, I always had my comb. But I didn't have any hair by then. They shaved my head bare at the orphanage. Lice. Scabs. It never grew back as beautifully. And the comb got lost. A few years ago, someone snatched my purse. And that was the end of the comb. Leolka said it was my own fault for taking it everywhere with me. But I couldn't bear to part with it.

That's tough, very tough, agreed Bożydar.

After the war my husband rescued me. We didn't have any children, but we never got bored. A child is a good alibi when nothing else in your life succeeds. Have you got children? she asked with feigned curiosity.

A son and a daughter. They work a lot. From dawn to dusk. My daughter-in-law got me my place here. She knows everyone. They're supposed to be visiting me when they get back from their vacation. I thought they were taking me with them. After all, they're going to my cottage. I bought and renovated it myself. It's so beautiful there. Surely I don't look like the sort of old boy who has to be hidden away in corners yet, do I?

No, you don't. Of course not. I have no children. Just a stepdaughter. She has a degree in pharmacy. She travels a lot. She works for an international foundation. She supplies medicine for people suffering from exotic diseases that are beyond Henryk's wildest dreams. Anyway, I've never had much affection for her either. She was impossible to love. When she used to visit us on Sundays, she'd be in a sulk the whole time. And she was highly adept at extracting money from her father. Only quite recently, at well over forty, she started writing to me. She's childless. That must be why.

She paused, and went on:

It's a pity she wasn't there in time. He was dying and he was waiting. He waited for her to the very end, she added.

After a long while she spoke again:

My husband and I were never bored. On Sundays we used to go for walks. We'd take a tram across the Vistula. We'd sit on a bench, and he'd ask: So what's a kreuzer, my little lovebug? You don't know. It's money. A coin. And have you ever seen a hoopoe? Never, not once, I'd reply. Not even in my dreams. And how do you spell capercaillie? With double L, I, E at the end, I think. You wonderful woman, if you go on loving me I'll bring you a welwitschia flower, my darling little lovebug. That's what he was like, she said with a smile:

Not very handsome. Quite skinny. In 1959, in the spring, he bought me a washing machine. He was given a voucher at work. Why am I telling you all this. I don't want to be depressed. Disconsolate. Although I don't neglect myself like the other widows.

Tell me, what's it all about? said Bożydar, leaning toward Helena. What's it all about? I've been a widower for eight years. Sometimes I feel as if my wife never existed at all. Then five minutes later they summon me to the phone, and I'm sure it's her calling. But that ought to pass. For some things not even senility helps.

He waved a hand in resignation.

Our memory likes to play tricks on us. The man who waters the lawn wanted to sell me a German invention: an angel's telephone. You know, for conversations with the deceased. Apparently this sort of cellphone keeps going for a year without charging. Because you have to put it in the coffin. But there's a minor problem, because the Germans bury their dead at a shallow depth, one foot at most. So it might not work here.

And you believe that? It's hogwash.

He laughed heartily. With his entire body.

She rebuked him for it:

He's handed out more than ten devices among the residents. The world has run ahead. We'll never catch it up. We are from ancient times. The young people are wiser than us nowadays. What do we have to offer them? A Council of Elders. A Council of Elders and Dumbers.

Ten devices. Who'd have thought it. So what, have any of them had a chat, at least? I'm curious to know: Is paradise all it's cracked up to be?

He was still laughing.

They've definitely had conversations. I'm absolutely sure of it. They go around being reticent but contented. As if they had a secret. But nobody owns up to it. What a band of egoists. They only ever brag about their illnesses. Whose is the more exotic? Whose is the more chronic? Whose is fatal? And which movie star had the same one?

But what would I have to say to my wife? Supposing I did get through to her on the phone, down there? What nonsense. She's a heap of bones. One time I dreamed about her. For a week I had very high blood pressure. A telephone for conversations beyond the grave. What a great business idea. People are always going to die. Jesus Christ, the simpler it is, the harder it gets. Some guy in America just looked at a stick and invented the floor mop. The dollars came pouring in. There's money lying in the street. You just have to know where to bend down for it.

In the street. You can forget about the streets. There are no streets here. I haven't been to the city for ages, said Helena, getting up from her chair.

She cast a weary look at her interlocutor and added:

Well, then? Let's meet tomorrow by the roses. After the priest's visit. I'll have them then.

Bożydar raised his head and looked her straight in the eyes.

Those roses are pretty. I once planted some on the balcony, ramblers, but the frost killed them. Though this year it's too hot for the roses here to last long. Their petals are already falling off.

They've planted those roses to stop us from escaping, she said, adjusting her wine-red pantsuit.

That's the truth. Thorns. Thorns everywhere. A mouse couldn't squeeze through.

But you could manage, couldn't you? One look at you and I know you could do it. Don't be mad at me, Helena, but you're still quite a looker. Ah, Cupid's dart, ever young and venomous.

She shrugged and said:

Essentially, if I wanted to, I could pack up and get out of here. Nobody's keeping anyone here by force, are they? I've escaped several times. I could pack up. Say a stylish farewell. And order a cab to the station.

But to go where? Where? asked Bożydar, without looking her in the eyes.

The end of life is still life, after all, she replied.

She glanced at Bożydar. He bowed his head toward the notebook. She caught his fleeting glance. His eyes were half asleep, dreamy or tired from the heat and the dust.

She struggled to her feet. Then walked surprisingly well, without effort. Leaning forward, as if the air were putting up resistance. And limping very slightly.

And I won't get bored in the winter either. I know how to make feeders for the birds. They're homeless too, he shouted after her.

She didn't turn around. But in the doorway she slowed down. Leaning forward, on bent knees, taking tiny steps, she went on another tour of the terrace. One leg after the other. Without lifting her feet from the ground.

In the passage she came upon Szymon. He was clinging to the wall. Tapping his index finger against it. Like a woodpecker.

The manager called a meeting.

The fine weather is good for walks, he declared, squinting into the bright sunlight.

You never know when it might rain. You never know, muttered Benia.

I wish to point out in no uncertain terms that five of the residents have managed to get past the gate.

The manager sounded tired. Weary of the heat.

I don't know how it occurred, but I have taken the appropriate measures. The staff already have more than their share of responsibilities. The police have a lot of work to do. While people are away on vacation, thieves are on the prowl. We've no time to keep driving to the precinct to fetch our residents—and when we do, they deny living here, and pretend they've never seen me before. That's particularly relevant to Helena, who has already been on the run twice before now. And she ran up some debts by traveling around the country. But she's childless, so who's going to pay me back? That is why, from today, every, I repeat, every single guest at our home is to wear a little sunflower armband. In a moment the caregivers will distribute them to everyone, and will help you to put them on. And may I remind the staff: appearances can be deceptive. Some of those in your care don't yet look like residents of our home, which is why I'm ordering you to increase your supervision.

It doesn't concern me anymore, bragged Benia.

I'll be going home soon. My son has finished the renovation.

He's taken a long time over it. It must be about three years now? said a caregiver, laughing aloud, as she put on Leokadia's armband.

Everything has to be top quality. My son doesn't like trash. I'll move in as soon as the last screw is in place.

Screw? Surely you mean nail. The last nail in your coffin, said Miron, sniggering.

The caregiver adjusted the material to make the sunflower symbol more visible. She stood up, and immediately turned her attention to Henryk:

Henryk, please go to the bathroom. Your incontinence pad needs changing. You're close to steaming. Benia, what's making you sad? she said, winking at her.

Is life so bad here with us? Was it better at your son-in-law's place? But we all know he hit you. Chased you outside into the snow in nothing but your nightshirt. And he wouldn't let you eat. But you're very well off here. Come on, give us a smile.

Only those with teeth can smile, remarked Henryk.

Why not show me a picture of your late husband? prompted the caregiver, sighing.

Benia brightened up, and nimbly searched her pockets. She pulled out a torn photograph.

The registrar let me keep it. I had to hand in his ID card. Do you want the picture? she asked. I nodded, and she ripped it off the card. That's why it's torn. But never mind. I'm glad I have it. It's like I'm always holding his face in my hands. Keeping it warm, trilled Benia.

He wasn't a believer. He couldn't be. They'd have closed down his workshop. I used to iron his shirts for Party meetings, but I taught our little Piotr to say the Hail Mary.

Helena was gazing indifferently at a resident with a harmonica, sitting nearby. He started to play when the manager stopped talking. But first he took out his dentures and placed them on a side table.

He played a jaunty dance tune. But he lacked strength and

air. To Helena it sounded as if the false teeth were snapping, applauding him like a hired claqueur.

Henryk, are you about to throw up? Are you feeling sick? asked the caregiver, seeing Henryk's face had twisted into a scowl.

What do you mean? I'm writing a poem.

Better and better. Not just a Consul, but a poet too. We're all ears.

She clapped her hands, plainly amused.

But don't forget to change your pad for me, she added.

Henryk began to declaim:

The bones of a woman found in the desert. A skeletal epigraph for the last supper. Phoebus's neon lamp changes skin into parchment like that of Saint Sabas.

He stopped.

And searched for the next line.

The caregiver laughed, waved a hand, and walked away, swinging her hips.

Like that of Saint Sabas, repeated Henryk, and went on reciting:

The blackened sandals . . . no. That's not it. Once again. Like that of Saint Sabas. The blackened straps of sandals walk by themselves to the Southern Star. As patient Jesus to Emmaus. Nothing about those.

He stopped short. And dug around in his memory again.

When will you die, when? Do you want to be burned or buried? asked Benia insistently, returning her husband's photograph to her pocket.

Give me a break. Are you going to wear an armband? asked Helena.

I've heard they gave you the bedroom left by the woman who died of pneumonia, the best one, with a balcony, remarked Benia.

Helena put the armband in her pocket.

I made a request, and they granted it. I couldn't go on living next to the treatment room. I could smell chlorine all the time. Chlorine, you understand? The same thing they sprayed in the railcars. You'll never understand. You weren't in a transport. You didn't have to lie on a stretcher with a rotting arm and smile for your photograph.

They gave you a new room, but I've been here longer. Once again you're better off. My husband was a cobbler. In a squalid little hovel, where not even the geraniums could survive, you remember? But as for that Master of the Arts of yours.

Benia, calm down. You're confusing me with someone else.

Helena wearily waved a hand.

Am I indeed? That's a good one. Confusing you with someone else, huh? You Jewish bitch. I can tell what sort of a creep you are. Just you listen: My better half died after twenty-four years in the job. He failed to make it to his jubilee. And in those days the Party gave anniversary rewards. For the twenty-fifth it was a vacation in Bulgaria. So I heard, don't you believe it? You always were non-Party, so it's hard for you to believe it. But it's true. A vacation, or a coupon for a Fiat.

Helena looked at Benia, who was purple in the face with rage. In several tops, a woolen vest, and a shawl, she looked like a little teapot steaming under its cozy.

We met here, Benia, don't you remember? Calm down. When I arrived, I gave you a small radio. A little battery-powered one. All right now? Are we friends again?

I got the radio from another resident, who only likes the television.

Listen, Benia, I didn't know you before coming here. Truly.

I couldn't give a tinker's damn. A vacation or coupons. For a Lada even. But he died. Less than a year before his anniversary. Just two months and four days short of it. Yes. Exactly. He was killed by fumes from the glue for sandals. Brain cancer. It was a bit like having the hemispheres soaked in glue. They curdled and boiled over. Don't scowl.

You're right, Benia, dreadful things happened to people after the war too, Helena agreed, trying to calm her down.

It's you that's had a quiet life. If you'd given it a good try, you might even have forgotten about the camp. I know what I'm saying. Your other half went on and on living. But he was always being ill, wasn't he. He couldn't get over it. And they cut out part of his stomach. Sometime in the 1970s. Then there was that asthma. Gallstones. He used to complain that you never cooked. You just doll yourself up in front of the mirror. He has to eat dry food. Dry food all the time, and that's why he's sick. After all these years, now I can say it—we had an affair. But I was a widow. I could have a frolic.

Benia pauses.

And then talks faster.

It hurt you, didn't it? A little beauty like you having to share your husband with a common skivvy. That little idiot Benia, who'd pit cherries with her own claws rather than buy a jar of jam and be done with it? But he was a brick: He serviced two women.

I never met the gentleman with whom you had that affair. I swear it. Nor you either. Give me a break, or my blood sugar will drop. Then I look terribly pale. Ugly. Like a sick woman.

Altogether it, he and I, didn't last long. A month or two? How much did we love each other? We didn't fear God. But then he broke up with me. From one day to the next. Without a word. Listen, I'll give you something to keep. I'll only give it to you. Because you haven't got dementia. You can remember everything, even what they gave us for breakfast yesterday. Or whose name is whose and what illness they have. Even the caregivers' names. And what the nurses' children are called. Once again you're better off, you see, she said, searching her pockets.

And smiled. She'd found what she was looking for.

Look at this cute little box. Fancy, isn't it? And here's a little silver basket with a lock of my momma's hair.

I won't accept anything from you. How do you know it's a lock of your momma's hair? You were two years old when you wound up in the orphanage. That's what you told us. Maybe you were trying to curry favor by making out you'd had as tough a life as ours.

It's my momma's. I've always had it around my neck. You envy me. You've never had so much as a piece of string around your neck. You never got anything from your momma. You invented that comb. Big deal, a comb. Now listen up: When I die, you can put it in my coffin. I mean, you will make sure someone does that, won't you?

I won't accept anything from you. I know why you're prattling away like that. You're sweet-talking me—it'll be the other way around. I'll die, and you'll be left with that box.

You always did know how to outsmart me. You lured him away from me. You knew all the tricks. You wouldn't let him leave you. Or let him be with me and have cooked food.

Henryk revived and said:

Attention, please, I'm continuing my recitation. Attention, my friends. Listen to me. Nothing about those who lost you. You saw birds circling above your face.

He came to an end.

He looked around. And rewarded his own poetic effort with applause.

I don't know you. We met here, said Helena, endeavoring to set things right.

Please, please, don't go telling me there's something wrong with your head and you can't remember anything. It's easy to forget the evil one has done to others. As if it weren't you people who martyred our Lord.

Sweating, Benia ran her fingers up her face. From her chin across her nose. She rubbed an eye. Reddened, it was watering.

All right, have it your own way, agreed Helena.

I'll put the box in your coffin.

Can you folks smell the sea? asked Henryk, feeling the back of his head. The veins on his temples were throbbing.

Nobody answered him.

I can always catch the scent of the sea. From afar, my friends. It's the invigorating air. Marvelous, enthused Henryk.

No, I can't listen to any more of this, screamed Helena.

For a while everyone was silent.

Apparently another person has passed on, said Leon.

Several people have bitten the dust, confirmed Szymon.

They're dropping like flies. It's too hot, said Miron, opening his eyes.

So what happened to that engineer who used to play chess with me? he continued, staring into space, the whites of his eyes reddened by the heat. His irises narrowed, like a cat's.

Heart attack. I think, replied Szymon, his face sullen, like after a scolding. Slowly, cautiously, he put the back of his hand to his cheek, as if testing his body temperature.

A heart attack. What a death, said Henryk, pulling a face.

A vulgar death. And very unhygienic. When you have a heart attack, your sphincter relaxes, and you end up lying in your own excrement, right in the middle of the common room before the entire company.

Henryk stopped talking.

His lip quivered like that of a skittish horse. He frowned, and got up, showing his well-made teeth smeared with bits of food.

A heart attack. Everyone always dies of a heart attack. It's lucky I have a tropical disease. I don't even know if anyone else in the world has it, he added with satisfaction. Then tensed in his armchair as the back of his neck stiffened and he felt pain all over.

I forgive you. I do, trilled Benia, looking in Helena's direction.

Anyway, my children didn't like him. A strange man in the house. And he was jealous of my son too.

But I think a heart attack is a fine way to go. Though personally I'd rather die as fit as a fiddle, said Leokadia, settling more comfortably on her lounger. Her lips moved in a nervous tic.

Die fit and beautiful, adds Helena, calmly now.

Even in my coffin I have to look good. There's nothing worse than a body crushed by other bodies. Piled on carts. Whole stacks of them. Gnawed by rats.

During a heart attack you certainly don't wallow in your own excrement, declared Leokadia.

A heart attack is so invisible. Wonderfully abrupt. Tell yourselves what you like. Just about any death involving the heart is graceful every time. Esthetic, without any of that horrible dying in stages. Like a tortured animal in a snare. The worst shockers of all are those protracted death throes of one particular organ, first it goes wrong, then it deteriorates, decays, ferments, but—so to speak—can't rot. Dying's all right, for sure. As long as it doesn't involve spittle, blood clots, or pus. It's better without any warning signs, she concluded. Quietly. In a childish tone. Then curled up like a wood shaving.

I'd want to stare death straight in the eyes, said Leon, wiping his glasses on the hem of his shirt. What the hell? In fact, I'm extremely curious about it. Being rapidly catapulted from this world would completely fail to satisfy my need for knowledge. If we must suffer for all these years, let's have at least some of the mystery revealed. I really am curious about it. That's why I can promise you that I'll be staring at death full on. Nothing will escape me.

It's a pity you won't be able to tell us what you saw, said Miron, laughing, and at once croaked:

I'm not interested in snuffing it the boring way either.

He stuck out his tongue, touched it with a finger, and clenched his lips.

I'm afraid there's nothing original ahead of us, ladies and gentlemen, said Henryk sadly.

The usual demise ascribed to old folks, a banal death from natural causes. In youth one might have expected some unexpected twists. A dramatic passing in unexplained circumstances, but now . . . We'll fade away and that's all.

What would you say to death under the wheels of a moving vehicle? said Benia brightly, but she at once grew sad.

But no cars ever come past here. And the delivery van or the Kiss of Eden hearse drive so slowly that it wouldn't work, an accident wouldn't work.

What about crimes of passion? said Helena, sitting up on her deck chair.

Murder in a fit of passion. I don't know about you other ladies, but I'd love to die at the hands of a violent, impetuous lover. First infidelity, and then death at the hands of a jealous man. What a wonderful death. Let him stab me with a dagger, with fury, with love, with madness in his eyes, right in the middle of my proudly presented breast. Would any of the gentlemen here be capable of such an act?

She fell silent, looking around the male contingent of those gathered on the terrace.

I doubt it, she added. And put on her sunglasses. Large. Plastic. Out of fashion.

One can only die with dignity on stage, said Anatol out of the blue.

He had a strong, throaty voice, like an echo replying from a well.

And even then it depends which role.

He stopped talking to wonder.

Because if it's about— he began, and to his own surprise broke off, on realizing he couldn't remember what he was going to say or what the entire company was talking about. So he nodded, and smiled to imply that his mind was concealing the mystery of the best, perfect repertoire for encountering death.

But all in all, better before an audience. Always better than alone, said Henryk.

Then at once, as if cut down, his head fell onto his right shoulder.

Here you have a first-rate audience, dear Consul. What do we have to do here, if not watch as the next in line from the home's cast of characters buys the farm before our very eyes? We've been presented with a fine show, and yet we're still complaining, said Miron, laughing.

Moments later he grabbed at his crotch and froze in pain.

What on earth are you saying? said Helena in outrage.

This place is an affront to everything.

Yes, yes. Any second-rate stage at a rundown little theatre would be better, added Anatol.

But I think our home is exceptional. Truly exceptional. That house by the lake, that's the really awful place, protested Leokadia.

That's where there's a long line for the chop. But it moves quickly, Miron struggled to say.

He felt as if someone were jabbing a needle into his crotch. He closed his eyes. And massaged his aching body.

Leokadia stuck to her guns:

This place has its own microclimate. Even Henryk admits that if you really want to, you can smell the sea. You can feel the most genuine breeze.

Yes, I can confirm Leolka's words. I'd like to go to the sea. A bit of iodine would do me good. I'd be sure to breathe better. The sea has always done me good.

Henryk seemed animated. Aroused, as before a journey.

What's the point of us going away. Being somewhere else. Nothing. A change of climate is no help against death, my friends, said Leon, taking off his glasses. The overdose of bright light made him squint.

Helena noticed his red, puffy eyelids. They looked as thin and fragile as Chinese tissue paper. Leon's expression was absent. Tired by heat, pain, and lack of sleep. To her own surprise she wanted to brush her lips against his burning eyes. Soothe them with a gentle kiss. She wanted him to take her by the hand, squeeze tight, embrace her, and stroke her hair.

The air is so good here, said Henryk, not discouraged.

A unique microclimate. It's not to be underestimated. That's why it's hard to get a place here, but not even the microclimate can protect against death. Yes, yes.

He paused, but at once thought of something else:

I've always had a nut-brown tan. I never, ever went as red as a lobster in the sun. It's all right for the riffraff to have a red tan. Not even in Africa. Even there I went brown.

He stopped talking.

He had noticed that his hands were trembling. As they always did when he felt strong emotions. That was why he avoided excitement. He appreciated routine, boredom, being half asleep, keeping his mind filled with safe reveries. Everything that calmed his hands also pacified his rapid, irregular muscle spasms and facial tics. Despite which he regarded himself as a dogged collector of memories. An addict, who couldn't get by without a fatal affliction.

He smiled. He'd remembered the end of the poem. He grunted. Pleased with himself.

Listen to the next bit of the poem. Listen. Quiet. Quiet. I'm reciting: Nothing about those who lost you. You saw birds circling above you. And Fate nimbly weaving a black thread into your gown.

He was silent.

That's the epilogue of an epic poem. Did you like it, dear Helena? And Fate nimbly weaving a black thread into your gown.

I guess.

That's good, because you were my inspiration. Though I'd like to stress in no uncertain terms that the heroine of the poem is not your wonderful self, but the skeleton of a woman found in the desert.

Henryk coughed into his hand. And wiped spit on his pant leg.

Thank you for the dedication, she replied. I've always felt I was a muse.

She saw that Henryk was trembling.

She held out a hand and gave him a friendly pinch on the elbow. An odor of feces emanating from the poet reached her nose. She moved back.

Dr. Josef. Such a handsome man. So clean, mused Helena. He had a lovely fragrance. A strong one. She wanted to be close to him, because then she couldn't smell the odor of burning human flesh that she was steeped in. He always had a perfectly tailored uniform. Neatly pressed. Showing off his figure. And polished boots. Shiny. Gleaming. He was so supple. So smart. He looked like a magician. In white gloves, holding an elegant crop with which he lashed his boot top.

She liked to stand before him. Raise her arms. Turn around in a circle. Again and again. She enchanted him. He'd fix his gaze on her body. He'd smile. And whistle a merry tune. Or sing. He was never in a bad mood. He'd watch her carefully. She felt visible. No one else looked at her. Nobody looked at her. Not even with disgust. Not even when she chased away squealing rats to dive into the heap of corpses and pull the bread out of a lifeless hand. She was always hungry. Despite the fact that the doctor made sure she was given milk each day before the injection.

Once she had read that in old age Dr. Josef liked to sit on the terrace of his Brazilian home. He listened to Beethoven. Read Tolstoy. Hitler's speeches. He loved apple strudel. He indulged himself. His dogs ate chopped beef sprinkled with raisins. He still kept medical notes. He jotted down diarrhea, migraine, chest pangs. He complained of tension headaches. Of rheumatism. Problems with his bladder and an intervertebral disc. He grumbled about frequent plumbing failures. He'd be standing under the shower, wondering why the water wasn't flowing from it. He didn't associate metal discs with holes in them with gas inlets.

Henryk sat up and said:

My dear friends, I'd also like to write an epic poem about the Emperor Tiberius' grotto. It was located in the southern part of the island of Capri, where the emperor was in the fine habit of swimming. Inside the grotto total darkness reigned. Blackness so intense you could cut it with a knife. But the most fascinating and terrifying thing was the acoustics. You could shout, pray, complain, and implore, but even the most piercing shriek was lost in the roar of the waves. No one would hear it. But if you put your ear to the wall of the grotto, touched the stone with your lips and whispered, every one of your words would be perfectly audible. Not futile. That's how instructions for the dead are spoken. What do you say to that?

Henryk took a few sips of water. He struggled to swallow it. Then glanced at his ruby signet ring. Thanks to osteoarthritis in the middle joint, he could no longer remove it.

A week later everyone was looking forward to cherries.

Once again their thoughts were of cherries, in bedrooms, the common room, the treatment room, on the terrace, and in corridors. They'd mention them while walking around, resting, queuing for a bath. Getting bored. Taking their temperature. Missing their families. Suffering. Looking at roses and anemones in vases. They talked of nothing but cherries. Each person's favorites: large with thin skin, small, sweet, watery. Stringy, tart, like sour cherries. Or light, white or also dark, purple, fleshy, almost mealy. Pretty, compact, a pity to eat them. Shapeless, pecked by starlings, gone bad, too moldy to eat, like a bitter, watery bladder. With tiny stones, flimsy peel. Or else huge, hard, well-padded with pulp, enveloping all the sweetness.

Henryk savored the memory of the mangoes he'd eaten in Africa. He'd describe the thick, sickly-sweet juice slowly trickling down his chin. But they always shouted him down: Cherries, our cherries.

Each person wanted to tell about the ones they'd had in childhood. The men boasted of the high trees they'd climbed. Quickly. Barefoot. Knees hugging a rebellious trunk. How they'd picked the fruits from the very top, while the branches shook, bending to the ground. The women fondly remembered twin cherries. They'd hooked them on their ears. Worn them with pride, like ruby earrings. They wouldn't let each other speak. Each one wanted to be heard. Once, long ago, he or she had eaten the best, the most wonderful cherries. From Grandma's basket. From Grandpa's rough hands. From Momma's lips. From Father. From a lover. A fiancé. A newly married wife. A stranger.

They were looking forward to their cherries. But meanwhile the dessert bowls were full of strawberry compote, rhubarb crumble, pear fool, and over-stewed apples sprinkled with cinnamon.

The manager strolled along the terrace increasingly often. He wasn't wearing suits anymore. Just white cotton T-shirts, carefully ironed.

What a scorcher. And it's only the first official day of summer. Well, girls, don't press your knees together. Air yourselves, air yourselves. Next year I'll install air conditioning.

He cackled.

And trotted off to his office. Waiting for him were the doctor who came three times a week, and the permanently employed nurses.

For three quarters of an hour they talked about constipation, ulceration, rheumatism, fecal incontinence, sleeping pills, painkillers, tranquilizers, heart medicine, anti-coagulants, tablets to lower blood pressure, to counter dehydration and swelling of the legs. They reported on things that were puffing up, swelling, bulging, suppurating, slowly bruising, or filling with pus or lymph. Who had something festering, burning, messy, slimy, soiling, peeling, stinking. Who had edema, who had clots. We don't cure, we just substitute, they said, repeating their principle. Sight with touch, bladder with catheter, hand with prosthesis, legs with walking frame. They considered how to provide everything to deal with gastritis, diabetes, paresis, the aftermath of strokes, fits, paralysis, or poor test results. They established who would do the bathing, washing, bottom-wiping, changing, trimming, and clipping, who would distribute crosswords, clean catheters, administer enemas, apply compresses, examine boils, abscesses, and peeling scabs. What had run out? Drops, ointments, suppositories, rectal enemas, vaginal pessaries, capsules. What else was needed? Bandages. Gauze. Dressings. Plasters. Pads. Swabs. Compresses. They agreed on the purchase of another set of syringes, hemorrhoid suppositories, tourniquets, dressings for varicose veins, boils, and slow-healing diabetic wounds. They established diets. Easily digestible. For diabetics. Those with stomach ulcers. Atherosclerosis. Kidney stones. The ideal menus for irritated gall-bladders. Swollen livers. Lazy bowels. They drew up a list of those to switch to intravenous feeding, on drips from tomorrow. They gave instructions about who'd be put into isolation. Who'd be put onto opiates. Who'd be given a larger dose of morphine. Whose family to inform. Precise organization. Detailed planning and implementation of set goals. All very important. The home had to run like clockwork.

The meeting was only briefly interrupted, when resident Leon Rabinowicz entered the office with an application for a dog.

They turned him out. Immediately. On the spot. Pulling faces, rolling their eyes, drumming their fingers on the desktop.

Leon's sixth application for a dog this month was rejected.

The other residents weren't asking for anything. That June afternoon they were entirely absorbed in covering pieces of card-board with cotton wool. Making new year's angels.

By now the summer had firmly donned its warm hat.

The world was melting in the heat. Sunshine came pouring from the turquoise sky. The blackbirds whistled with all their might, hopping from branch to branch. The geraniums, cyclamen, and dahlias were almost blowing their boxes apart with their roots, blooming and stretching toward the sun.

The heat was pouring down, settling in the treetops. Planted beyond the fence, they dangled their boughs above it, providing shade and respite for the residents. The air was thickening. Shuddering and pulsating. The movement of particles in the heat distorted colors and shapes. Whatever one's vision tried to recognize eluded it. As if whirling, refusing to form a whole.

After lunch most of the residents dozed in their rooms. The sisters remained active. Helena was helping Leokadia to get dressed. Despite lacking a left hand, she was more agile than her sister. She found movement less tiring.

The bedroom stank. It felt cramped and dark. Cluttered. Plates, small glasses, and vases were wrapped in newspaper, books and albums of nature in plastic bags. Just as if the move were not yet over.

There were pictures leaning against the walls. Watercolors depicting bunches of wild flowers. Pages from an old herbal, sepia prints in pine frames. The glue had gone dry and was crumbling. The plants had faded. It all bore witness to days in the past, in the summer months, when Leokadia would roam the meadows, fields, and gardens in pursuit of balsam, aspen, and German knotweed.

She'd pick dandelions, wormwood, and great yellow gentians. She'd dig out aniseed and wild ginger seeds, and spend four days making jam with them. She'd track down coltsfoot and wormwood, to warm herself in winter with absinthe-flavored liqueur.

Her friends most eagerly looked forward to the ointment she made from water violets. They weren't easy to find. She'd hunt for them on the muddy banks of ponds. Pools, canals, drainage ditches. Standing water. That was where the pale lilac flowers with yellow centers most often bloomed.

Leokadia would take off her shoes and wade. She liked to get as many leaves as possible. They weren't easy to pick. Hidden under the surface of dark water. Then she'd use a wooden stick to pound them in a large pot, adding a spoonful of buckwheat honey, and then pack the resulting paste into dark, pharmacist's jars.

The recipe was Georgian. Failsafe for skin problems. Burns. Psoriasis. Unexplained eczema. The ointment served Helena well. The German prosthesis was still reliable, and pleasing to the eye, the color of tanned skin. But the surviving part of her arm chafed beneath the plastic fastening. Was this the reason why, since their stocks of water violet cream had run out, Helena increasingly often went about with an empty sleeve, fixed to her side pocket with a safety pin?

Just like now, as she bustled around her sister, tripping over the picture frames.

I hope to hang them up one day, said Leokadia, excusing herself.

Then I'll feel almost like at home. The manager said that if everyone wanted to hang their pictures, after their demise the walls would look like a Swiss cheese.

Every one of Helena's visits began with her sister saying the same thing. Leokadia hoped that at least today Helena would visit for longer. She was always in such a hurry to get to the terrace, to that walking of hers.

Lean forward. Just a little. I don't want to yank you, asked Helena, helping Leokadia to put on her dress.

Somehow she was managing to do it. She did her best not to look at her sister's body. A starved body. Puffy from poor kidney function. Scarred by subcutaneous hemorrhages, overgrown moles, and bruises caused by injections and catheters.

Such lovely pictures, Helena. It's a sin to keep them on the floor. But what can I do? This isn't a home, it's a waiting room for the guillotine, complained Leokadia.

She liked it when her sister took care of her. Helped her to put on her underwear and dresses, rolled up her sleeves, straightened her collar, or smoothed the material creasing on her hunched shoulders.

A waiting room? That's a good one. Don't even say such things. Imagine you're at a holiday resort. Anyway, tell yourself whatever nonsense you like. If it makes you feel better to let it out. Won't this dress be too warm, Leolka?

I feel cold.

But there's a heat wave.

It hasn't warmed up for real yet. I'm sorry I didn't buy more of the dresses that button up at the front, I no longer have the strength to pull them over my head.

Helena began to cough.

Leokadia was quiet for a moment. Then, looking at the empty sleeve of her sister's dress tucked into her pocket, she asked her:

Are you going to wear your prosthesis? If your skin is chafed, there's ointment for bedsores in the treatment room.

Give me a break, interrupted Helena.

She folded her sister's nightdress. And tucked it under her pillow.

All in all, life is just one long line for the guillotine, said Leokadia, starting up again.

I've always felt as if I were eternally waiting for something, while people walk by, busy with their own affairs, without so much as a glance at me.

She broke off.

Helena started to cough again. She was suffering. Struggling to clear her throat.

You've an ugly cough. And it's not like Miron's. He wheezes from the larynx. He must be one of those disgusting smokers of tobacco or, God forbid, a pipe. You've got something in your lungs.

She stopped talking while Helena endured another fit of coughing.

You've an ugly cough, Helena.

Did you ever hear of a beautiful cough?

Perhaps the doctor should examine you, my dear. Examine you professionally? Listen to your heart to check for murmurs? It's strange, because after the war you never fell sick. I had everything: colds, tonsillitis, flu, all sorts of infections, sinusitis, and others, but you were never sick. All winter you'd run around without a hat or scarf. Just a beret and a neckerchief, and you never caught cold. Nothing. But now there's this cough. I don't like it. It hurts just to hear it. It thuds in your lungs. You look as if you're about to fall to pieces.

And I am, I swear it. I'm being blown apart by your comments. What rot you're talking. You're persuading me I'm sick. It's just a cough like any other.

Helena was distinctly tired.

As long as the manager doesn't notice, said Leokadia with concern.

It's a cough. It's nothing. Everyone gets them. Even small children. They cough all the time. It's treatable. What about your calcified veins? You'd do better to think of yourself. Let each take care of themselves.

You're right, said Leokadia, nodding.

I'm not having much fun. It's the hypertension. I can't bend over, I can't get excited.

Helena had noticed that lately her sister had changed. Despite her excellent dentures, the lower part of her face was sagging. She looked like a puppet torn from its strings. Instead of going pink from their daily rest on the terrace, Leokadia's complexion had taken on a waxy, dark yellow tinge. Her ceramic teeth looked as if they'd been placed in the jaws of a mummy.

It's a good thing you help me, Helena. The caregivers have no patience. They're rough, and my arm always gets tangled in my sleeve. I can understand them. Young people shouldn't work here. I can see it in their eyes as they're washing me. This floppy body, wobbling like jelly. They feel as if they're seeing their own destiny. A terrifying destiny.

Stop it. And then you're surprised I don't like talking to you?

Please let me say my bit. Who am I to confide in if not you?

Leokadia grasped Helena by the hand.

Don't you think about it? she said, almost in a whisper, as if fearing her sister's anger.

I don't recognize you, Leolka, you've never talked so much, said Helena, trying to pull her hand free.

You've become so out of date. Sentimental. Downright pathetic. Stop feeling sorry for yourself or they'll stamp on you, can't you see? Remember the platform? Remember how they chased us? That German told us to flee. And we ran. Quickly, like little animals. Fast. Faster. That's why we succeeded. If we'd taken pity on those who stayed behind. If you'd thought about Momma. Your legs wouldn't have carried you so fast. If.

Stop it. Please stop it now.

No, I won't stop. I won't stop until you become the girl from the platform again. The brave little girl who dragged me over the cobblestones like a rag doll. And then into the forest, then across the field. And even when they caught us and put us behind the wire fence, so what? So what? Life is like a waiting room, what an idea. It's so absurd. Common. Lousy. I don't know why you're telling me this. Am I supposed to pity you? Or myself? Why would I? We've had the great fortune to be alive. Can't you see? Last year on my name-day someone wished me to live to a hundred. The Consul, I think it was. So he wants me to give up the ghost quite soon. I can talk about it and laugh. Ha, ha, ha. You see? I'm never going to stand in line for the guillotine. Ha, ha, ha. See how it makes me laugh?

Helena pretended to laugh, then laughed for real, and finally started to cough. She calmed down.

Don't worry about me, Leolka. It's just a cough. Death will have a tough time when it comes for me. I'm going to get out of here anyway. I'm already making a plan. Don't sulk. I'll take you with me. But don't refuse me, like last time. It was because of you that I came back. Because of you. I'm still attractive. I could settle down. With someone who'd take proper care of me. Tell me how beautiful I am. Take me to the milliner, wait patiently on a hard chair while I tried everything on. And every Saturday I'd bake teacakes with raisins and sweetened carrot. I'd take you to live with me. But I won't find anyone here. No way. All these men. Horrors. Yesterday, the one with the walking frame and the dressing on his ear kissed me. Can you imagine? As a surprise. He asked if I'd seen the nurse who distributes the drugs. I stopped to think about it. And then he leaned forward. And right on the cheek. Almost on the lips. Luckily he judged the distance wrong. He missed. He surprised me. With a walking frame. So speedy.

Do you recognize yourself in your body? I don't, asks Leokadia, sounding like someone who's lost in a strange city, wearily wandering, circling, and constantly ending up in the same spot.

Give me a break. We must buy you some face cream.

Helena squeezed Leokadia's hand, and she responded with a weak grip.

Cream. Why would I want cream?

She burst into genuine laughter.

You talk like the caregiver. Yesterday I gave her a shopping list. I do want some good cream. That's all. Period. And some English talc for my skin.

Suddenly Helena hiccupped. She covered her mouth with her hand. She turned away, wanting to leave the room now.

Those beets were quite tasty, don't you think? she heard her sister say behind her. Trying as usual to stop her from leaving.

It's a good thing they don't serve too much meat. Even the best bit of roast pork smells bad to me. The one we had yesterday. At lunch.

Roast pork. Are you thinking of those meatball-patty things coated in goo? scoffed Helena.

I'd like to eat roast beef again, Leolka. Just one, rare, skillfully cooked piece. With a pickled gherkin salad and slices of red onion. All in a honey and garlic sauce. Our husbands loved those Sunday recipes of ours. I'm sure we'd be thinking about them as we ate, wouldn't we?

And without waiting for an answer, she continued:

How odd it is, yesterday when I went to bed I suddenly thought of my pink hydrangeas, I wonder if they survived the winter? The people who took over our allotment garden looked to me completely new to gardening. And they haven't answered my letters. I simply asked them for a photo of the dear little summer house. Taken from the veranda.

You don't know what people are like, Leolka. I'm sure they're coping very well. They definitely poisoned our mole. I'm sure that, of all people, they were the ones who did away with it.

Helena could feel increasing pain in her hip. She'd been standing in one spot for too long. She turned around again, and quietly, perhaps more to herself than to her sister, said:

Come to the terrace right now. Yesterday you never got up again after lunch. And the supper was very good too. You shouldn't lie around in bed so much.

I'm afraid to go out. More and more often I stay put for so long that I forget to go to the toilet. And it's always too late. Henryk is able to control his bladder. What's more I get the impression the caregivers, one in particular, scrupulously take note of who's needing more help. They're so devoted to the manager. As if he rewarded them for it.

Please, I beg you.

Helena, aren't you afraid?

Of what now?

She pretended not to understand.

You know what.

Leokadia laughed shrilly.

Helena shrugged.

The main thing is not to neglect oneself.

Leokadia interrupted her sister:

You know I don't like to talk about it. But tell me, Helena, why do you keep telling everyone you were Miss Auschwitz?

Helena pretends not to have heard the question and says:

Well, so what if you're afraid. So what. We were all afraid then too. I heard what the manager said to the delivery man: There are plenty of folks in here who were in the camps. It's not so easy to finish them off.

She waved her hand. The movement proved too abrupt, and her elbow hurt.

She went out into the corridor. She sighed with relief. She could no longer smell the odor of urine mixed with dust. They should air the mattresses more often, she thought, as she rubbed her wrist. She noticed that her fingers were looking more and more like the rhizomes of couch grass that were spreading ever more avidly between the paving stones on the terrace.

Where exactly are we? asked Henryk, opening his eyes.

He must have slept a short, deep sleep that gave him a tight feeling in the chest on awakening.

Where are we? he repeated, goggle-eyed.

Can't you see? Here, where we never dreamed we'd be, replied Helena, drawing beards onto some prepubescent boys in the newspaper.

Miron glanced at his watch. He breathed on its face and wiped it with his cuff. He smiled in satisfaction.

The caretaker called me a rather tasteless name, complained Henryk.

He called me an emasculated macho. I was a consul in Africa. I have a right to the best care. My daughter assured me the standard here would be the best. My retirement.

Tired out by talking, he clenched his lips. A scowl crossed his face. Of discontent or pain.

So what did you do to make the caretaker? asked Leon in a languid tone. He didn't feel like finishing the sentence. He sucked the tip of a dirty spoon and stared sleepily at his plastic bowl full of vegetable purée. The supper had gone cold. The mashed carrot was coated in a dull skin.

I can't hear you. You're speaking too quietly.

What did you do to make the caretaker? shouted Miron.

What did you do? What did you do to make him. Do you still not know?

Henryk interrupted, mimicking him:

What did you do? What was I likely to do here. I was taking a walk. What did you do. And what did you do. I must take walks. If you don't keep walking, you just hop into bed and it's all over. Welcome to the house by the lake.

And I think you defecated by the gate, said Helena calmly, without looking up from her drawing.

What on earth are you saying, said Henryk indignantly.

Just what I saw. What we all saw. From the terrace.

Now Helena was putting on her sunglasses, too large, a bad fit for her shriveled face.

Szymon walked past the table. There were whole days when he didn't notice the others. He didn't respond or address anyone. He held a dialogue with himself. Usually he quoted accounts of the final moments of the residents' lives.

Today it was no different:

The festering liver shows in the small yellow eyes. Puke that's come straight from the blood stream. Huddled in her own piss. She pissed like a cow. Lots of it, frothy. Mouth open, tongue lolling, blue, stiff.

He stopped talking, and gazed at the sugar bowl.

He carefully folded a dishcloth, and walked off, muttering.

The way he plods along, said Helena irritably.

It's that plodding that has the worst effect on my nerves. There's always someone plodding around here. Haven't they got decent shoes? Each morning, on my way to the dining room, I find slippers all over the place. Single ones. Down-at-heel. Nothing but odd ones.

We're all odd ones here, said Henryk.

He closed his eyes. He gripped the armrests of his chair tightly with both hands. He was wearing a suit, once well-cut, but now it hung off him. The material was frayed and worn smooth.

That's the gospel truth, the gospel truth, agreed Benia.

My world is over on the other side now, said Henryk with a whistle.

The world of the living can no longer compete with it. The

other world is calling. Populated by those one wants to be with. That helps one to lose the habit of life, said Henryk, nodding.

Well, then? asked their caregiver.

I hear you're still plunged in inconsolable grief for those left behind? I'll read to you after washing, but on condition it's not as muggy as yesterday, she said, taking away Henryk's bowl of cold carrot.

I haven't eaten yet. Nothing yet, he mumbled in dismay.

We're closing the kitchen. Come back tomorrow, Henryk, for some milk soup.

With a deft movement the caregiver unfastened Henryk's bib. She wiped the table top with a cloth.

Helena waited for her to leave. Only then did she speak:

I hate being a widow. Although I don't neglect myself, like other women who've lost their husbands. I think I'd have preferred to pass away first. Leave someone inconsolable. But as usual, I've been left behind. Alone. And it's coming up to night again. I'll want to stroke him on the cheek. He's not there. Disturbing the darkness is in vain. Reaching out in the gloom. All we have left is to stick a finger in the space vacated by whoever has passed away.

When my husband died, I wanted to die too. Though he wasn't good to me, said Leokadia, sweating profusely, and examining her hand covered in brown spots.

So what did the ungrateful fellow do to you? asked Henryk, hiccupping, and staring at his own fingers. Short, wide fingers, with rough, chewed nails.

He drank, and then he took it out on her, replied Helena on behalf of Leokadia.

Ah, that's quite normal. There were two of those in my family, said Benia, moving her hand as if polishing the table top.

Go on, tell them, what do you care. They think that if they have tropical diseases from Africa they're the tops. Tell them, said Helena to encourage her sister.

There's nothing to tell. It's all in the past. Tomorrow I'm going to see our lovely volunteer, she'll take care of my poor hands. She did my feet beautifully.

Then I'll tell them, said Helena decisively.

Please, Helena, I don't want everyone to—.

In vain Leokadia tried to stop her sister.

He made her dress up in a striped uniform and drilled her, reported Helena.

Stop it, he was sick with alcoholism. And then—

Leokadia's voice cracked. At emotional moments she lost command of it.

If he had a disease involving intoxicating liquor, that's quite another matter, agreed Henryk.

Partial or total incapacitation. Tomorrow I'll tell you the relevant articles of the law for it. I have a disease that's pretty much undiagnosed. I doubt five other people in the world have it, he boasted, leaning his head back.

I forgave him. One must forgive. Otherwise one does harm to oneself, said Leokadia in a hushed tone, which gave her better control.

I forgave him. I looked at him lying in his coffin. Pale. As if ashamed. So defenseless. My heart was torn to shreds.

She fell silent, and put a handkerchief to her perspiring neckline.

Forgive a man like that. It's hard to imagine that he had higher education. Though I'll admit all dead people look so clean. Neat and tidy, said Helena, leafing through the newspaper in search of pictures to color in.

A hush fell that she didn't like. But this summer even the crickets were making less of a noise in the grass.

I'm told you were an actor, Anatol, why don't you ever say anything? she asked, addressing a man who was lying still on an unfolded deck chair. His face was so pale that it looked as if drenched in milk. He resembled a canvas dummy dressed in a linen suit.

Why are you so obstinately silent? Why don't you talk to us? she inquired.

Because I don't feel like it, he replied in a booming voice that didn't match his shriveled, bony face.

But why not? All of us here admire you. We're longing for just a little chat with you. You're our star. Our beloved heart-throb, urged Helena.

I don't like making myself hoarse to no purpose. I did enough speaking on stage. Seventy years in the footlights. And all those interviews for the press. Pre-premiere, post-premiere.

The women must have gone crazy for you. Personally, I'm not surprised. Fifty years ago you must have been handsome.

I used to give the ladies a touch of Hollywood. Beautiful farewell kisses. Their thighs were as sweet as apricots. The girls were like that once upon a time.

Anatol broke off. Diving into the past must have caused him unexpected pain. Perhaps he'd bumped into an uncultivated part of his memory.

Could you remind us which movies you were in? I've always been so fond of the television, you see, said Helena encouragingly.

In the days when Anatol was performing the television hadn't been invented, said Miron, laughing.

I liked the radio best of all. You didn't have to clean your shoes for the broadcast, admitted Anatol, without showing a trace of emotion.

His face remained immobile. As if carved out of crumbling limestone.

My daughter makes movies, said Henryk.

She was such a pretty little girl. I'd tell her to tie her bow and we'd go to the park. I'd sit on a bench, and she'd be in the sandbox. How I loved to watch her. A little girl with fair hair, a tiny nose, shapely, and her little ears didn't stick out. She was always a good student. I never knew what it meant to have to make a child do her lessons. Or math. She brought home nothing but top grades.

He stopped. He looked at their faces. As if seeking confirmation whether he could carry on.

And when she put me in here, how I wept. I know, it's a shame to admit it. I cried. Even so she fastened my seatbelt angrily. And then she said I hadn't taken care of her either. But there were the English lessons, the pool, the physical therapy. She went everywhere. And I didn't play with her in the park because I was so fond of watching her. From afar. I'd be sitting there. I could see her bow on her little blonde head, and I'd be so happy.

Henryk looked toward the garden.

A cat was unhurriedly strolling across the lawn. It stopped, the tip of its tail quivered nervously, and it walked on.

Did you know that our minister's widow fell down the stairs again? And yesterday she fell off a stool, said Benia, making a gesture as if polishing the table top.

How did she get onto the stool? That one has brawn, said Helena enviously.

Leokadia gazed at the garden.

How beautifully it's burgeoning this summer.

In August I always took her to the seaside, continued Henryk.

And every Sunday, when it was warm, I took her to the lake. She swam from the age of five. I taught her myself.

His gaze was motionless, dull. Like a blind man waiting for the bus.

At night there were always frogs. Toads. As big as stones. How afraid she was, he said pensively.

Benia started up again:

That minister's widow is always getting up on something, or falling off of something, but she never breaks a bone. She must be made of rubber, as they say. Apparently she never worked in all her life?

I had an earplug made of rubber. Its effect was that you didn't feel like smoking, boasted Henryk, looking at Helena.

She was putting on some orange lipstick. It emphasized the coarse fair hairs on her upper lip. He followed her every gesture, watching expectantly. Like a dog at his master's table. In the hope of a morsel.

What did you have made of rubber? asked Miron.

An earplug. An earplug. Are you deaf, or what? A Swiss colleague gave it me as a gift. He was posted to Africa too. If you wear this sort of rubber earplug, every cigarette prompts nausea. Just think, how did that technical idea advance in the West? A small rubber stopper battling against a powerful, global addiction.

Henryk, did they call you Gammon? Yes or no? said Miron, laughing.

His laughter soon changed into a throaty cough, and then he spent a long time spitting out phlegm.

Henryk didn't answer. He stared into space. His gaze took in the old apple trees growing by the fence. They were bearing small, wild apples. The boughs hanging from their short, stocky trunks looked like the limbs of a cuttlefish. Below them, fallen fruits speckled with mold lay rotting and fermenting in the sun.

The sky had cleared.

It had changed from gray to dirty pink, then at once azure, becoming a transparent dome, above which the sun could live it up with impunity.

It was a very peaceful hour.

The volunteer had gentle, fluid movements. She even seemed a touch languid. This suited Leokadia. Nobody had ever touched her feet. Including her husband.

This emboldened her.

Everyone's jealous of my implants, chirped Leokadia.

My teeth are like pearls. My husband was a dentist and an oral surgeon. A double specialty. He adored his profession. He could spend hours discussing materials for molding bridges. He'd tell me the little tube for draining saliva was airlocked. And he'd have to buy another.

So how did you meet?

I was yawning while waiting for a tram. He came up and asked if he could take my picture.

He fell in love. At first sight, said the volunteer in raptures.

He merely wanted to take a photograph, explained Leokadia calmly.

My left incisor extended beyond the alignment of my bite. It's not common, at least not in *Homo sapiens*.

Have you been here for long? said the volunteer, massaging her instep. Leokadia found the touch of her hands very pleasant, despite the latex gloves.

A few years. One can get used to it. Although when I left my apartment, my furniture, spare bedding, vases, tapestries, table sets, my souvenirs from the seaside, from the mountains, I thought that once I got here, and had to live empty-handed, without all that, I'd die very soon. I loved my three little rooms, the hall with the round window, the wide kitchen windowsill. Pigeons used to come visit me. They liked pearl barley the best. Each morning I'd make myself a cup of tea and watch them eating. I used to overfeed them. How I fattened them up. I couldn't control myself. Always a few handfuls too many. Out of affection. That's how we had breakfast together. Me and my pigeons. I liked the early morning silence in the house. Altogether I liked the quiet life. I wasn't drawn to cafés. Helena, my sister, is quite different. She was always painting the town.

Does it hurt when I use this pumice?

No, not at all, in fact it's rather nice. My heels are my real Achilles heel. It's hard to take care of them when I can't bend down, said Leokadia, smiling.

The volunteer worked in silence.

Leokadia was enchanted by her hair. Heavy, luxuriant, thrown back on her shoulders, lightly fastened with a metal slide. Leokadia envied it. In the past she'd had similar hair. In the camp. Slightly curly. Soft to touch. Even after the experiments. Every morning she'd step outside the barrack and shake it. Emitting a cloud of gray powder. The air was full of it. It got in her mouth. All from that smoke coming out of the chimneys.

Perhaps you'll tell me some more? prompted the volunteer.

Leokadia shuddered.

Well, and it was only after I'd fed my pigeons that I'd go wake my husband. I never think about what they're doing now. After all, I couldn't bring them here with me. I couldn't. I know you're going to laugh, but sometimes I weep for them. One of the residents here, Leon, brought his palm tree from home. He takes care of it, wipes the leaves, talks to it. But you can't bring pigeons. They say that on arriving at these places people die quickly. Even those whose mental state might make you think they don't know where they are. But they're not indifferent to it either.

That's awful, said the volunteer, putting down her nail clippers.

Leokadia smiled.

I was hoping it would be the same for me. But it wasn't. I'm alive. I'm still alive.

I heard you were in a camp? The manager said so, she added, bending forward with a nail file.

Ah, just for a while. It was a very long time ago, it doesn't matter now. Why talk about it. Do you know the manager well? He's so awfully dutiful.

A very nice guy. He's able to enjoy life. But it's not easy, especially after what he's been through. Did you hear—his son died. He was only a few months old.

Yes, but we folks here keep on and on living. And somehow we can't die. He has to look at us. It must be painful for him.

Isn't it too warm for long sleeves? asked the volunteer.

I always feel cold. When it comes to the weather, I'm like an Italian.

Why cover up the tattoo, when it sticks out whenever you move anyway. Apparently Helena has her number on her thigh. You're shapely compared with her. It's hard to believe you're twins. Though if you look closely—

She broke off, leaned forward and blew away specks of nail filings.

I have a tattoo too. A dolphin on my ankle. I'll show you when I'm done.

How can you bear to touch old people's feet? You're so young and pretty, asked Leokadia quickly, wanting to change the subject.

Somebody has to do it. It must be my destiny. At school we were told that in those concentration camps—

Leokadia hurriedly interrupted:

My sister, Helena, is very careful not to neglect herself. I'm glad I'll pass away with beautiful feet. It's not nice to walk around paradise with corns.

You won't be passing quite so soon. It's not so easy.

Will you paint my dear little fingernails too? Are you married? asked Leokadia.

No, not yet. But in fact I might be, soon.

And are your parents still alive? What am I asking! I'm sure they're alive and well. You're so young.

My dad's not alive anymore, she replied without sorrow.

The way things worked out, my mom and I moved to another city. I was only three or four at the time. And then. I don't really know if he looked for me. He didn't visit. He never wrote. Or sent a Christmas present.

What about you? Did you look for him?

Not until last summer. I didn't get into college, I was bored and I thought: What have I got to lose? I'll find his number and give him a call. A little girl picked up. Maybe my sister? So I asked: *Could I speak to Mr. such-and-such?* There was silence at the other end. But I could hear breathing, I knew the girl was still there. Finally she replied: *Well, not really.* So I asked: *When can I call to speak with him?* And she said: *You see, there might be a problem. Because Daddy's dead.* How stupid is that. At first I couldn't care less. I even thought how bright that little sister of mine is. And I went on to say: *Since when?* As if that could change anything. And after a long silence, the child, more and more terrified, replied: *Since three years ago.*

The volunteer swallowed hard.

All right, let's see if the massage has relaxed your hands.

She raised Leokadia's hand to the sunlight. They both saw how smooth it was from the cream. Pampered.

Sometimes, even very early is already too late, said Leokadia. Happy that the brown marks on the back of her hands weren't so visible anymore.

What about some nail polish, would you like that? suggested the volunteer.

A lock of hair had slipped from under the slide. It fell onto her face. She didn't brush it aside.

Red, said Leokadia in delight.

Yes, red.

That's nice. But maybe it's not appropriate. Better the colorless Pearl.

But why—the red suits you.

Really? said Leokadia, smiling, and added:

You know, I used to be a brunette. A fiery brunette, as they say. They used to tell me I should be in the movies. You know what, my sister and I were both very pretty. I'll tell you a big secret. For years and years after the war I couldn't admit it. But now, when I have a good day, I'm not afraid to talk about it anymore. Listen up: I'm a year older than Helena, but on the ramp Daddy said we were twins. Because word had already gone around that they were very keen on twin girls at the camp.

Leokadia broke off. She looked at her hand against the light.

I like the red, it's nice.

There, you look so elegant and feminine. Now it's your sister's turn. I'll wait for her. We've time before tea.

She won't be coming. She never lets anyone touch her. Not even the doctor. But I can't take my eyes off this nail polish.

Ever closer to its height, the summer was gaining strength.

In the mornings it was bearable, but later in the day heat came pouring from the sky, so they hid in their rooms, seeking cool air.

By now the visiting priest had finished celebrating the May masses, but the shrine of the Holy Mother of Jesus that stood in the garden was still decked with ribbons. As the hot wind stirred them, the Virgin Mary became the Mother of the Orphaned, the Supporter of the Sick, the Citadel of the Exhumed, the Ark of the Devotees, the Consoler of the Suffering, the Temple of the Suckled, the Gateway of the Infirm, the Lodestar of the Meek, the Bride of Those Departing, the Reason of Those Entering, the Queen of the Martyrs.

Helena watched as they gave an airing to the residents on IV drips and those who had to be tied to their chairs—they hadn't the strength to sit up on their own. Those who were excessively emaciated had pillows placed under their hip bones, allowing them to rest outside for longer. A window in the centenarians' room was even set ajar.

At their own request, out of boredom, two of the female residents had volunteered to sort the laundry. They were sitting face to face, holding the clothes up to their eyes to read the embroidered number belonging to each of the residents.

Are you ladies packing?

A man with a naked torso, in nothing but a pair of shorts, sat down beside them. His body looked devoid of muscles. Loose gray skin thrown on some bones.

Remember, only take what you can carry. Two bags, not too heavy. They'll herd you along. Quickly, quickly. That's what one woman divulged to me. They've already taken her. She's a goner. And she was smart. She knew everything. Everything. So just what you can carry in two hands. Not too much.

Apparently another one passed. In the night, said Leon breathlessly.

But so beautifully. In their sleep, so beautifully. One can only envy them, he added, watching with curiosity as one of the residents spoke fondly to a bowl:

Eat up, look, what nice food. Go on, eat up. I've no time to keep on and on asking you.

So who's the poor eater? asked Leon. But as if feigning curiosity. Artificially. In a weary tone.

Filek. My little puppy dog. Come on, eat up. See how the man's looking at your bowl? Any moment now he'll have your food. Go on, then. One-two, and the bowl's empty.

What a nice doggy, praised Leon.

You can't see him, but he really was a nice little dog. Please believe me. He had a bit of Pekinese in him. A short little snout. Eyes like saucers. He was so clever. And so handsome. Almost a pedigree. They put me in here, and he went to the shelter. But I was too weak to walk him. Eat up, see what nice food? Chopped egg and beef. What do you think, does Filek remember me?

Leon didn't answer. He went off to his palm tree.

My little Filek. He sat with me all day in the window. He had his own cushion. He was a picky eater. Only in the park, when he saw other dogs, did he eat up at once. That's what my Filek was like.

It was a long time since July had been as generous and as cruel.

Stifling heat settled on the walls. It felt as if the insides of the building were swelling, and the space contracting. Pressing.

Come, like infants let us tarry, Close to the heart of Mother Mary, hummed Benia.

If life's toil bedevils us. Come, come at a trusting gait. With tearful eye and wistful heart. The heart the children's voice doth know, it turns aside the painful blow, she sang, rocking herself.

More and more of the residents are asking when the violin trio is coming to perform again. One of the violinists was pale with black hair. Thin as the Host.

You folks can't remember what day of the week it is. But you have a perfect memory of what happened on July twenty-second last year.

The manager was sweating, red in the face.

But, ladies and gentlemen, please don't get in my way and don't prattle on about sonatas and other such musical ecstasies. This year there won't be a concert. The artists are not coming. I pay a high price for the performance, but before it's over half of you are asleep, and the rest are coughing, spitting out phlegm, squirming in need of the toilet, or scraping your chairs.

It's quite impossible to hear the music, confirmed one of the nurses.

She removed a thermometer from a resident's armpit. Without so much as a glance at it, she shook it and put it back in a container on the medicine trolley.

You could have a temperature of forty-two degrees and they

won't even notice. But my daughter promised me that the medical services here were of the best standard, whined Henryk.

Henryk, please don't start bleating. You can still sit up, and I've so many folks with bedsores, said the nurse, rapidly turning back to the treatment room.

Helena was satisfied. Thank goodness there wouldn't be any concerts this year. Dr. Josef would have liked that dark, skinny woman. He always listened to music with his head bowed. Dreamily. He didn't close his eyes. Nobody's presence bothered him. She would watch him. She'd lie on the stretcher carried outside the barrack, where the light was better for photography. The stink of feces, of rotting flesh. A piece of skin hung from her arm. The photographer stood over her. Blood was leaking from her like sticky syrup.

Dr. Josef would devour her with his gaze. And she'd look him straight in the eye. He was pleased when she played with him. He had chosen her for himself. This girl would bring death on herself, and he'd help her in this game.

Henryk didn't want the volunteer to care for his feet.

But he was happy to be helped with a manicure. He let her cut his fingernails and trim the cuticles.

You have no idea how solidly I sleep. What is there to do here? He laughed quietly, pleased with himself.

What can I do? I even nod off on the terrace. There's no one to talk to. Except perhaps Helena. You know the one. The Auburn-haired Comforter of Men Agonized by Prostate—that's what I call her. I've always had a weakness for redheads. They called my wife the Squirrel. Not in my presence, of course, but I knew anyway. An attorney has to have a seventh sense. My better half really bloomed in October. Her russet hair went well with the crimson leaves. But she was beautiful all year round. Though in Africa, where we lived, as you know, she was sick for a month, the heat was bad for her. She was beautiful against the snowcaps in Karpacz. She came out splendidly in the photographs wearing a highland sheepskin coat. She looked good in a bathing costume. She had fine bones. In summer she avoided the sun, and her face was like a china doll's. Whenever she came to see me at the office, my colleagues were thrilled by her. She knew how to dress. Subtle ways to show off her breasts, the line of her calf, her slender neck. She was always reticent. One of those melancholy women who are described as enigmatic. Of course, it's great luck that they remain sparing with their words to the end of their days, saving us disappointment.

Henryk laughed softly, bashfully.

Her childhood nickname was Squirrel. She must have suffered a lot because of her red hair.

Suddenly he fell silent and let his head droop.

The volunteer thought he had dozed off—his hand had gone weak, but the moment she stopped filing his nails, he opened his eyes and said:

You know what, she had an abortion. In fifty-two, at a doctor's in Pułtusk. She said that because of her wartime experiences she felt incomplete. It seems they did experiments on her. And instead of multiplying. Regenerating. Forgetting about the war, about corpses. Having something that would strengthen her connection with life, she took herself off and had an abortion. She filled herself with quinine. I came home from a meeting with my colleagues from the court. She was sitting on a stool in the hallway, very pale. She confessed what was up. I was furious. I'd had a few drinks. I pushed her in the belly. She had a hemorrhage. She showed me the toilet bowl full of pink water. All in silence. With her head drooping. Like an insincere funeral guest who's afraid she might show a cheerful face. Like one of those Jewish hired mourners. As I've said, she was always reticent. She didn't like caresses. Being touched. She didn't want to sleep with me. Only on days when it might result in a child. Because she did want one, very much. So why did she have an abortion? When it could result in a child, she made a vegetable salad that she decorated with pickled mushrooms. I knew this supper was a sort of invitation. Then I'd go visit her. Her room was long and narrow, ending in a window that was too small. She chose it herself. She insisted on it, although it was the darkest and ugliest in the house. But nothing doing. Nothing doing, every time. Month after month. I was starting to think maybe I was firing blanks, to put it colloquially. And when a man has those thoughts, it's never a good thing. Even in bed he doesn't feel like it anymore.

He broke off, chewed his lips, licked them and continued:

After the abortion, after the hemorrhage she never let me near her again. She refused. Anyway, once she reached forty-seven it was too late.

For a while he fell silent and slowly scratched his cheek.

Once I slept with the daughter of a woman I represented at a trial. I was involved with the underground in those days. I defended workers who'd been fired from their jobs. My client's daughter came to my office to ask if her mother would be out in time before her child was born. I realized that the father of the unborn child was not present in her life. He'd gone. Taken fright. She had nothing to live on. There she stood in front of me. Young. Abashed. In trashy clip-on earrings like the white buttons from a quilt cover. Her pregnancy hardly showed, but when I looked more closely, her flowery dress was already hugging her. I don't know what came over me. I threw myself on her like an animal. And she didn't resist. She was quiet. Submissive. Like a robot. Like my wife. Just as indifferent. But the whole time, consciously or not, she kept stroking my hair. That involuntary or shameful caress went deep inside me. I wanted someone to be just like that with me. I wanted my wife to touch me like that. I longed to feel her hands on my head. But she— All her life she carried a vial of poison inside her. Her childhood was like arsenic. Talking about or even just hinting at her childhood years could cause the capsule to break and release lethal toxin into the organism. Ah, what nonsense.

He waved a hand, twitched his nose as if to stop it from running, and continued:

That adventure with the young girl gave me hope. One night I approached my wife from behind. Her nape was pale and fragile. I'll never forget those tiny freckles. The color of rust. Almost invisible. I took her hand and plunged it into my hair. She leaped back. Terrified. She was breathing fast, fearfully. As if I weren't her husband. But someone strange, an intruder. She used the hand that was meant to caress me to cover her mouth. I knew she'd found out what I'd done. That I'd betrayed my own betrayal. With the thing I longed for. There was something in her eyes. Some flashes of satisfaction. Gratification. As if she knew about the betrayal, but couldn't care less. I couldn't any longer. I couldn't hold out. I began to weep. Like a big scolded child. A spurned orphan. I spent a long time sniveling. At the top of my voice. I couldn't stop. I cried for myself. For my poor self. As I was sobbing away like that, half-lying on the kitchen table, I noticed that she was looking at me. Watching. She wasn't scared anymore, or even satisfied, but indifferent. A spectator. A bored observer. An unfeeling witness to my crying. I don't know how long it lasted. The whole performance—as she called it. Put an end to this pitiful performance, she said. She turned away, looked at herself in the sideboard glass, and tidied the hair above her brow. What do you want? she said. I'm your wifey. No one else. Just your wifey. Are you still feeling bad, tell me. Feeling bad? What more do you want. She fell silent and started thickening the soup with cream. "Wifey." That word didn't suit her. Primitive. Crude. It soiled her lips. I never forgave her for that. Never. And although I could sense that her icy chill had to be from that invisible vial of poison, I couldn't forgive her. Not even now. When she's gone. I often think about her. When she threw herself out of the window, it was all the same to me. I went about furious. Half-cut. I had no one to cook for me. Finally I found someone. A woman from the countryside with a small child. The little girl. I adopted her. I treated her like a daughter. She was pretty. Fair, almost amber little plaits. She was afraid of frogs, just like a child. As for my wife, it's strange she never gave me any sign that she was going to do it. No hints. Not a shadow of grief. Everything as usual. The laundry, the cleaning, the cooking, looking through the albums from Africa. She liked taking photos. She was good at it. No elephants or giraffes, more intimate detail. The glance of a dealer in ebony figurines, some rotting fruit, a milk tooth found in the grass.

Perhaps those were the signs, said the volunteer.

What do you know. Her final sentence was: "Don't forget to

collect your coat from the laundry tomorrow." She killed herself on a Tuesday. The neighbor phoned my office. As if I'd been hit hard right in the solar plexus. I had a sweet metallic taste on my tongue, like when your mouth fills with blood.

He fell silent and swallowed hard several times before speaking again.

Helena, the one with the make-up, told me there are never any signs, never. When they really want to go, they don't leave any signs. They want it to be entirely without trace. We're the ones who demand explanations, we stalk our dead, we analyze their final days and nights. They've gone long ago, but we cling onto them tightly, we don't want to let them go, set them free. We demand words from them. We want to hear them. We believe they're watching us, we end up interpreting banal, everyday events as messages from them.

Helena seems to have had a tough life too. It's a good thing you told her about it. Perhaps that'll make it easier for her, said the volunteer.

I've never told a soul. Not a word. Just you, because you'll be leaving this job in a month, won't you.

I'm transferring to the next home.

The one by the lake?

I don't know of a home by the lake.

I get it, I get it. You're bound by a rule of silence.

There was a short pause.

But how did Helena know all that about your wife? For her to answer you that way.

She didn't know anything about her. She was just talking about her husband.

But they were so happy. They went places by tram.

That's just it, he didn't leave any clues either. Nothing. Once it was all over she found out he'd refused treatment. And he'd had a chance, there was hope. The cancer was discovered at an early stage. The doctors gave good prognoses.

Yes, it's strange. Once death is in our vicinity, everything's different, said the volunteer.

She squeezed out a dab of cream. In circular movements she rubbed it into Henryk's hands.

You know what, I went to a psychiatrist. When I got to the age of forty. I thought to myself it was time to be done with it and start to live normally. Move on. Live for tomorrow. For silly things. Doing the accounts. Going to meetings. No, I'm not a madman. I'm a normal person who doesn't have a normal life. A normal life. But when that doctor asked me what a normal life is, I couldn't answer. He had trouble with me. He gave me something to help me sleep. Why do I need sleep, being asleep is even worse than being awake. It was Leon who finally helped me. He said a normal life is not having an abnormal life. And then I understood that I've already lived one life, and now a second one has started. Though it's not perfect either. But I'm resigned to it.

There you are, your hands are as pretty as a picture.

The volunteer had finished and was satisfied.

Thank you, my dear child. Has anyone told you how very nice you smell.

With evident difficulty Henryk reached into his pocket and extracted a hundred dollars. The banknote was crumpled. Soiled.

Straight after that he dozed off. Calmly and soundly. As if he'd completed a plan he'd had for ages. The volunteer looked at his gaunt face. The moment lasted a short while, until his breathing became quiet, almost silent, perfect. At that point Henryk opened his eyes and smiled.

Keep your fingers crossed they won't serve us goop for supper again, he said, clapping his hands, and groaned as he tried to get up from the couch.

The temperature was rising by the day.

Helena scratched one of the caregivers who tried to cut her hair.

The other residents too seemed excited by the sudden eruption of summer. They went for chaotic walks, to and fro, aimlessly. They passed each other without speaking, jostled one another, or waddled in single file, without knowing who was following whom, why or for what purpose. Their actions were perfectly gratuitous. They served no end apart from the act of moving.

Some of them were lying down, warming themselves in the sun like lizards. They huddled on deck chairs, as if they'd nodded off. Only a tongue poking out from time to time to moisten lips testified to wakefulness.

There were also those who, with a determined expression, filled the hours by folding tea cloths and towels.

Now and then someone laughed to themselves. The cackling seemed unreal, disconnected, not tied to any situation. But nobody reacted to it either.

Some listened to the conversations as if they were being held in a foreign language.

The manager walked about the terrace. There were damp patches of sweat beneath his arms. The heat wave had driven him out of his office. He was sorry he hadn't installed air conditioning. He always grumbled in the same way when the weather was hot in June.

Do you want to be burned or buried? asked Benia, blocking his path.

He shooed her away with a firm gesture. Like an annoying fly.

She shambled onward. She hitched up her skirt to the waist, squatted on the steps down to the garden, and took from her pocket a slice of bread sneaked from last night's supper. She broke it into tiny pieces, as if for the birds, and put them in her mouth. She couldn't remember where she'd left her dentures.

Most importantly, the baby jackets. Made of linen. With straps, she said, lisping.

My bubbas looked so cute in them. My mother-in-law gave me a little tin bathtub. I bought a little rubber duck at the general store. They liked to splash around. The neighbors brought me so many diapers. Almost forty flannel ones. And cotton calico.

I was never interested in having children who turned out well. I didn't want any, said Helena. I don't fit in with other women.

Henryk sat more comfortably on his deck chair and said:

And I have immense respect and admiration for the womenfolk. You've always been closer to death than we men. You took care of the deceased. You washed the bodies of the dead. You combed their hair. You dressed them for the coffin. You were mourners too. You sat by the graves. You tended them with genuine passion and devotion. You wove wreaths. You are courageous. But as for me, I'm endlessly afraid. But so what. We can't spend too much time wondering what now. We might start to regret that our mothers gave birth to us.

We had a good life. The whole village was like a family, said Benia.

They even loaned us meatballs for the children. And poured a little vodka into our glasses. All for all. I toiled away and I was in good health. But now I ache all over, because I don't do anything. Being idle is like an invitation to the next world. I'm telling you.

She nodded, emphasizing each sentence this way.

What about you, do you want to be burned or buried? she quizzed Helena.

Who shuddered. She seemed to be staring at the shadow of the trees receding into the depths of the garden, toward the rosebush hedge.

I'm not crumpled, am I? she asked, turning around.

She smoothed her skirt. She flicked off a speck of dust that wasn't there.

Not in the least, Benia assured her.

She put a piece of stale roll on her knee. Squashed by her outspread hand, it crumbled easily.

That's why I wear angora. Always looks freshly ironed. Maybe not right for summer, but it's cool. I don't neglect myself, like other widows, declared Helena, moving toward a lounger.

Since her last escape, when she'd broken her hip, she walked slowly, without tearing her feet from the ground. She left her crutches in her room, and whenever the caregivers pointed this out, she muttered that they added years to her. Despite physical pain, she was in constant motion.

Benia was intently pressing breadcrumbs into her pocket. She wasn't listening to Helena. No one was listening. Only Leokadia. Though she knew it all by heart.

Helena continued:

After my husband's death I had plenty of gentlemen callers. Nothing but highly qualified professionals. Attorneys, doctors, even the retired chairman of the Supreme Court. But they won't march their way into my heart. It was my husband who was my drummer boy. He alone knew the rhythm of my heart. I shan't mention him again. A love like that only ages you. These days low-calorie romance is in great demand.

She ended her speech, standing over a lounger.

She was wondering if, after lying down, she'd be able to get up again.

Benia was licking her lips. Chapped. Covered in tiny scabs from clenching them.

Suddenly she made a noise that sounded like ripping the plastic packaging off glycerin suppositories. She could also mimic the residents' voices. The squeaking of mice. The groans of the caretaker's unoiled bicycle. The whistle of the wind tugging the rooftiles. Deathbed wheezing. The sighs of those who took too long to die, effortlessly, lightly, unhurriedly. As if from nothing but being confined to bed.

Do you want to be burned or buried? she repeated quietly. To herself.

She lay down on the lounger Helena was standing beside.

Nice weather, said Leokadia dreamily.

Time to be off to the allotment garden. You can't imagine what a lovely little summerhouse we had at ours. Made of stone, yes indeed. From the rubble thrown out when they rebuilt Warsaw's Old Town. Such a dear little garden, sweet strawberries straight from the bushes. And what wonderful cherries. Three little trees, and whole buckets of fruit. I'd be off there. Right now. Just as I'm sitting here.

You have an allotment garden here, grunted Miron.

Leokadia looked toward the rosebush hedge.

We're almost in July. Or is it July already? There are sure to be blueberries.

And spruce trees. With little green paws, agreed Miron.

Every year I picked the newly grown tips. You have to pick a kilo or two. Pour spirit over them. Add a spoonful of honey to the shot glass. It's good. Healthy. It'd revive a stiff. Best in the fall. But September's a long way off. That'll be the day.

He fell silent. He scratched the smoothly shaven back of his head.

Helena stopped, leaning against the frame of a deck chair. She watched a resident in a wooly hat with a pom-pom. He was cutting playing cards. From one pile to another. And back again. Gnarled by rheumatism, his fingers slid over the greasy surface.

After the war I was afraid to eat, she said quietly.

I used to hide bread. Like you, Leolka. But I was lucky, I came out of it. Why reminisce. Although we're told now is the best time for reminiscences. Do you know—we won't be seeing our Truda on the terrace anymore. She won't be eating with us. Yesterday they started feeding her through the nose. But it won't last long. A hungry stomach starts to eat itself. I feel sorry for her. She was so amusing. She was always telling us to pack because the Germans were coming. Pack up. Just what you can carry in your hands. She was so amusing. Who'd have thought—through a tube. And she always had such a good appetite. Not like me and Leokadia. Just what you're able to carry. The Germans are coming. Any minute now the Germans will be here.

Helena sighed. And fell silent. She moved along the ellipse of the terrace. With clenched lips, stooping slightly, as a way of reducing the air resistance. She cooled down, once again distant, proud, attentive, focused on each successive step.

She kept walking, patiently following her line of sight. Her skull was becoming damp. Sweat flowed down her face, deviated on her jaw, and slowly trickled down the wrinkles on her upper chest.

You were afraid to eat. What on earth are you saying, Helena? said Leokadia, rebuking her sister.

You've got some bad dreams into your head. And the doctor told you not to reminisce. At the orphanage too they kept saying it never happened. It was a dream. Give it a rest, she said, watching her sister as she walked. Simply looking at those stubborn knees struggling to bend made her feel exhausted. Not so long ago Helena had reminded her of a cat. Wild, agile, always darting off in elongated, light bounds.

Miron was cleaning his ear with a cotton swab.

Leokadia is right. Why go on about what did or didn't happen. Why the hell yammer on dolefully. There's nothing I want more than dementia. That's the best medicine for a fucked-up life.

What a thing to say, said Leokadia quietly.

But I must admit that actually amnesia is the best thing for old age, she agreed after a pause.

Dementia, dementia. Dementia, not amnesia, shouted Miron.

And instantly fell silent, examining the wax he'd dug out of his ear.

That's not true, whispered Leon.

If you don't have your memory you have nothing. I have the memory of the little blue bowl my wife liked to drink her tea out of. Even when we had guests. She insisted. You have nothing. The memory of that butterfly. It sat on her nose. A white one, it matched her dress, I managed to take a picture. The corridor in the hospital. She pinched me for courage, I wasn't at all afraid. The argyle sweater. She brought it back from the DDR on our twentieth wedding anniversary. It itched on the neck, I often wore it to work. She told every joke from the end, but I laughed anyway. She kept repeating them, over and over. I'd pretend I'd never heard them before. We liked to laugh. Together, very loud. She never washed the dishes, she didn't like doing it. I'd be angry, and she'd be angrier. She always beat me at tennis. I'd be quivering with rage, while she'd hop over the net and throw her arms around my neck. That's what she was like.

He broke off.

He wanted to say more, but he had to hold his breath to allow the pain in his chest to ease. He leaned over the table. From this distance the table top was no longer a uniform white, but covered in a gray cobweb of bits and pieces.

And what I'd like most is to have my teeth back, mused Benia, stroking a slice of bread.

What fine teeth I had. Leokadia, that dentist husband of yours never saw the like.

Stomatologist, not dentist, said Leokadia, correcting her sister without taking her eyes off her.

He had a master's degree in stomatology. I've told you so many times before. My husband. I'd have liked him to visit me, come and cheer me up. But he was in such a hurry. He didn't wait for me. He died. What can you do.

As white as snow. All of them, every last one was white, and there were still so many of them, they hardly fitted in my mouth, recalled Benia.

Sometimes I felt as if I had three rows of teeth. And they were so pretty. With a charming gap at the front. A lucky gap.

Nice weather. Time to be off to the allotment garden, mused Leokadia, trying to straighten her torpid legs, but her knees felt too heavy and her thighs too weak.

She watched Helena making a second round of the terrace. She noticed the beads of sweat. On her chin, on the tip of her nose—like peas.

You have an allotment garden here, hissed Miron, cleaning the other ear with the same cotton swab.

Helena paused to settle her breathing and then said:

Each morning at the allotment I liked to listen to Beethoven. Only very recently I read somewhere that Dr. Josef liked him too. At night the earth steamed, and from dawn I'd listen to Beethoven. And I never thought of Dr. Josef at all. But as for that man in the uniform, I was always thinking of him. Still so very young. The German who saved me. His collar chafed his neck. I noticed a red stripe. Odd how a child remembers everything. What matters and what doesn't alike. He looked me in the eyes and shouted. Told me to run for it. Us two and our father. Just the three of us. Daddy, Leolka, and me. That German. He gave us three weeks of wandering in the woods. Is he still alive? Definitely not. He must have been about twenty years older than I was.

She nodded, as if confirming her calculations. Tired, her voice shook. She wanted to lie down, she could feel that the heat was melting her powder. In which case perhaps she'd better return to her room to tidy up.

And what would you do to that German, huh? If you were to meet him here, say? wondered Miron.

There are two possibilities, Miron. Either I'd look him in the eyes. For a long time. Without dropping my gaze, to avoid God knows what. Or I'd hit him in the face. For helping me to escape, she concluded, rubbing the balustrade with her open hand.

Szymon came onto the terrace.

What a fine summer we're having. Birds squawking. Head exploding. So many beetles. Enough to make your foot ache from stomping on them. So hot the sweat goes trickling down your butt. And as for nature's vile odors. All that stinking stuff that's supposed to be blooming. I tell you, it'll all be rotting very soon. Rotting as you watch. Go bad and drop off. Every single leaf, flower, beetle, or ant. It's all going on the compost heap. Like us, on the compost heap, he finished, gratified.

It's true, Szymon. A bracing, sunny day. Ideal for the allotment garden, agreed Leokadia.

She watched as Szymon struggled to raise a mug to his lips. Seeing this effort, one would think everything he touched weighed a ton.

A marvelous day. My momma had one just like it for her funeral. The sun shone for her one last time, recalled Szymon, licking his lips.

Benia craftily rummaged in her pocket. She took out some candy wrappers, bits of fluff, threads, gallstones, and crushed geranium leaves. She examined it all as if trying to remind herself what exactly she was looking for.

Apparently that's bad. Better if it pours, she said.

Better to have heavy rain. A sign that the Lord God is weeping for the deceased, because he was obedient to God. He was not a sinner. He lived well. Properly. He didn't break the commandments. No hellfire awaits him. So was your momma burned or buried, dear Szymon? she asked, smoothing a fold of her skirt.

Momma was such a good woman. There were so many people at the funeral. The entire board of my company. And all so beautifully dressed, in suits, the women in black, with their hair up, every single one, said Szymon, gazing at the fleecy geranium leaves.

So you weren't crushed by grief for your momma—you noticed everything. Even the women's hair, said Miron, laughing.

And at once began to cough. He expectorated with difficulty.

They bought beautiful flowers, said Szymon, nodding.

He raised his mug again.

Large, artificial bouquets. Easy to clean. I used to dip them in a bucket with detergent and they were done. Clean. Such lovely flowers. Just like real ones. Luckily the gravestone is under a willow tree. In the shade. The sun is so bad for the colors. There was no vodka at the wake, my friends. I couldn't do that to Christ. No vodka, no alcohol. Just rhubarb compote. And cold meat as well, wonderful meat. They ate it all. And they finished off all the horseradish.

He fell silent.

He drank water in tiny sips, then put down the mug dangerously close to the edge of the table.

Miron laughed and said:

Whatever you like—horseradish is a handy first-aid kit for any mourner. It wrings out a flood of tears. However much you hated the deceased, the first hint of horseradish will have you crying like a baby.

Szymon stood up straight, stiff as a poker. He opened and closed his hands.

Or like a river. Do you cry like a baby, or do you cry like a river? Benia quietly questioned herself.

Szymon waved a hand and trudged off toward the common room.

He couldn't do that to Christ, he couldn't do that to Christ, sneered Miron, watching him walk away.

What sort of a guy have they brought us here? Momma this, Momma that. A shitty momma's boy. I bet Momma croaked as soon as she realized what she'd given birth to.

He laughed, the cackle quickly changing into coughing.

For several minutes he choked, and then, exhausted, took a long time to calm his breathing. His reddened eyelids were watering, so he wiped them with the back of his hand.

So you see. That's a fine way to behave. Christ has punished you for bad-mouthing your neighbor, said Benia, removing and reinserting the things she had dug out of her pocket.

He's no neighbor of mine, snapped Miron wheezily.

Helena was about to start another round of the terrace.

When I was fifteen Christ was present in my life, she said.

I was always crossing myself. Even in front of the clock. I had to cross myself four times. Twice in this direction and twice in that. We were living in the orphanage run by nuns. I was afraid that if I didn't cross myself, they'd split us up.

She fell silent. Her face tense and alert, she took the first, hesitant step.

Give it a rest now, Helena. Those reminiscences and walks. Neither of them does any good, Leokadia reproached her.

Better take a look at these flowers opening. And only yesterday the buds were so tight shut. I've seen a lot of little blue beetles already. Were they born now, or did they hibernate under the moss? They go marching around the place. All their beetly life they roam around like that.

I used to be like that too, said Helena.

I remember how I'd put on some less than flattering footwear and off I'd go. The main thing was comfortable lace-up boots. With a hard leather sole. No rubber bottoms. I'd walk around the city for hours. As soon as I had a problem or a worry—one, two, and I'd be out of the house. I walked my troubles to death. One has to be brave. Always very brave.

She smiled. She was silent for a while, as if a memory had occurred to her.

Leokadia smiled and said:

It's true. I forgot to tell you something. Yesterday a ladybug sat on my skirt. And she—

You told us, you told us about the ladybug, Miron interrupted her, tapping his forehead. All day you went on about the ladybug, the same thing over and over. Ladybug this, ladybug that. Enough to drive you nuts.

There used to be such fine women, said Henryk dreamily, with his eyes closed.

He fingered the hairs protruding from his nose. He stroked his own cheek. Slowly, steadily. As if lulling himself to sleep. He didn't stop whispering:

You could talk. Have a conversation. Those hints. Smirks. Flirting. Word play. You got heated up. You soared. Higher than the birds. What is there to discuss. The romances of our youth. All flown away.

He half opened his eyes. He took his hand from his cheek. For a while he examined his fingers. They were narrow, refined, but the nails were chewed short, to the quick, giving them a blunt look.

You are so romantic, Consul. It's unusual in a man, said Helena, going up to Henryk.

Yes, so you think, my dear. But maybe one should forget that one used to have a heart. Come to terms with the fact that now there's nothing left but a muscle in its place.

He gripped Helena's hand.

He kissed it and said:

Though when I look at you, I grow wings again. You, Helena, are balm for a tormented soul. Balm, and a woman, of course.

Helena smiled.

Thank you for the compliments. I like them very much. I don't want to be treated like a shriveled sack that used to be a woman.

Henryk scowled. He let go of her hand.

Why are you making that sour face? You have no idea how hard I have to fight for them to let me keep my long hair. Naturally, it's best to shave it all off and run a wet soapy sponge over it. You'll save on shampoo. What harm do my curls do them?

But actually I haven't talked about my dear little ladybug, Miron, protested Leokadia.

Miron waved a hand.

Now it's ladybugs and more ladybugs. On and on about bullshit. Those ladybugs are enough to make you throw up.

At once he tired. He began to cough dryly.

I remember perfectly, I haven't uttered a single word, insisted Leokadia.

How long she sat with me. A tiny little ladybug. As if she were my dear friend. I know it sounds irrational.

She laughed.

But that's exactly how I felt. She sat beside a button on my skirt, just here, and she was fine. She wasn't in a hurry to go anywhere. In a way it felt so nice, you see. You know what I mean, don't you, Helena? You understand me.

She paused.

No one spoke. Nobody was listening to her.

Helena trudged on.

Miron was watching Henryk, sitting opposite, staring off to one side and tugging at his earlobe. This activity was absorbing all his attention.

I felt so close, Leokadia continued.

So very close to it all. I stopped feeling afraid. Musing. About the fact that I'll be gone. That the earth will suck me in. Dissolve me. Grind me up.

Nature is one big blender. It minces. Processes. Spits out, said Helena, nodding. She stopped to look at her bright red fingernails in the sunlight.

But I felt so good with the little ladybug near me, Helena, said Leokadia, smiling.

What a lovely summer. The summer will be fabulous this year. Truly. I've got a feeling. I'm curious to know if they've put plastic bottles over the delphiniums. The mole will destroy them like anything. Dear friends, you won't believe it, but we had such a lovely little mole at our allotment garden.

She went quiet, suddenly upset.

Be content with recreation, folks. Recreation. Listen to our Consul. He came here to take the air, said Miron, nodding.

The fresh air, said Henryk to clarify.

Do you want to be burned or buried? Benia asked no one in particular.

She looked up and glanced toward the entrance gate

If only my children knew how strong I am again. They don't have to do a thing for me anymore. I can stand without help. On one leg even. For almost fifteen minutes. Because now I eat well. Three times a day. And the doctor examines me. But I'm not sick. No, she repeated, chomping on a finger with her bare gums.

I'm so robust. There's no need to walk alongside me. My grandson is still at school. I could help. Make pancakes. Liver and apples. I was never lazy, never. Once everyone had gone to bed, I did the ironing and put things away in the closet. I made the soup for tomorrow. I was a very good housewife. I filled four scrapbooks with recipes. I baked every kind of cake. And bread with fennel seed. The dough always rose, it never sank, she warbled, rapidly, without thinking, rubbing her sticky hands together. Like a fly.

So where was our Consul yesterday? He didn't join us for breakfast. No one to lift him out of bed, huh? Or perhaps he was having a roll in the sack with one of the little nurses for hard currency? mocked Miron.

I had to spend some time in the treatment room.

Why, did your blood pressure rise sharply? laughed Miron, and Leokadia agreed:

Blood pressure, yes. But Henryk, at breakfast today you looked so purple. I know what sudden rises in blood pressure are like—they make life impossible.

I forgot who told me that you've always had a problem with your blood pressure. That's why they called you Gammon.

Miron was about to snort with laughter. He suppressed it, swallowed too much air, and suddenly started to cough. Too hard. He huddled up, clutching the armrest of his chair.

Slander. You degenerate. You old degenerate, replied Henryk, squeezing his eyes tight shut.

A nurse appeared. She was making her round. She came up.

With a swift, nimble gesture she wiped the saliva from Benia's lips, and placed a blanket behind Miron's back.

Do you want to be burned or buried? Benia asked her.

And stroked the spot where not so long ago her right kidney had been.

The nurse didn't reply. She went down into the garden, sat on a deck chair and exposed her face to the sun.

Do you know what I want? If it ever happens. I want to die in good health. In perfect health and not neglected, said Helena, and burst out laughing.

They can burn me and scatter me from my balcony. I had such a nice view of the yard. Onto a little bench and a children's jungle gym. Every year the bed below was full of red flowers. The housekeeper always planted it out. I'll be all right there.

And I'd like to be scattered in a store with chic dresses. I like to dress up. I could live in a boutique that sells wedding gowns. Even when I'm dead it'd be nice to be among those veils, said Benia, clapping for joy.

And they can fling me around a honky-tonk. As long as there's dancing every night, said Miron decisively.

Tangos, for example. None of that twirling. The slower numbers, so you don't get short of breath. They can scatter me there. Straight down a busty broad's cleavage, he added sadly.

Henryk was outraged and spat:

But you simply can't do that. It's illegal. If everyone had themselves cremated and scattered wherever they liked, what on earth would happen? We'd be wading up to our knees in ashes.

Anything's possible. You can do anything, Henryk. You just have to pay the right person. Press a bit of cash into their hands and the problem's solved, said Miron, and laughed. Hollowed out like a willow tree, his body emitted a dull, stifled snigger.

As he gazed at Helena, Henryk calmed down. He liked watching her face. Regular features, eyebrows tinted black, prominent cheekbones. Her gestures. The way she narrowed her eyes.

The way she walked. The way she *smoked* her ballpoint pen. The slow, sensual hand movement, the parting of her lips, and the calm but deep inhalation of *smoke.*

Time to be off to the allotment garden. Such fine weather, said Leokadia, adjusting her hat.

Look, Helena. Take a look around, please, she urged her sister.

I know, I know. It must be beautiful at the allotment garden by now, she agreed mechanically. Almost with anger.

Watching her, Henryk noticed the tension in her face, while she stared to one side, pretending to be unaware of his glances.

Leokadia carried on:

The neighbor's bees are sure to be zooming around the flowers by now. I wonder if the new owners have gotten rid of the flower-beds. They said they were going to lay grass. My God, grass. The years we spent sweating over those seedlings—all gone to waste.

You have a garden here, replied Miron, choking and wheezing.

Finally he sighed, and the wart on his nose rose and fell. He leaned back in his chair. With a languid gesture he wiped his eyes. He began to undo his shirt. His hands seemed clumsy, barely able to disentangle each button, then ponderously pushing it through its hole.

What dreadful heat, said Henryk.

He made a sweeping gesture with his hand, as if to make everyone aware of the heat prevalent around them.

Can you hear? said the woman clutching her purse to her chest like a child, addressing Helena.

Can you hear that? It's starting. Where are they going? They must be thieves, huh? Good people stay at home.

Helena agreed.

The city was buzzing. She could hear it clearly. But to Helena its presence was the same as the sight of a kite gliding above the high fence surrounding the grounds of the home. She could only imagine whose hand was holding the string.

It was like that at the library. In the late 1950s she'd received her compensation and the prosthesis. She wanted to join the living. She started working. She laminated new books, wrote out the registration details, and glued together old copies. The library was downtown, and the noise of the city got inside it in the form of a monotonous, terrifying roar. She felt as if she were shut in a large jar. The hours piled on top of each other, one exactly like the next.

During this time, those days from the past never let her go. The sunny morning when Dr. Josef shot the old man who had come to say goodbye to his son before going to the gas. Dr. Josef had spotted him in the hospital waiting room. He asked why he'd come here. As he listened, Dr. Josef slowly undid his weapon. He shot the man straight in the head. Then, furious because splashes of brain had soiled his uniform, he killed two little girls too, Mufka and Szlamka, who were waiting to be measured. She was sitting in between them. In choosing his victims, he'd looked at her too. She hadn't moved. Bang. Blood. The nurses threw the old man into a wheelbarrow, put the children's bodies on top, and carried them off to the pit.

She didn't like working at the library. Her colleagues didn't talk to her.

The kike woman is pretending to work. She got compensation from the Krauts, and she makes out she's so unfortunate. But she smells of Soir de Paris or something like that, though it must be from the second-hand store. She doesn't smell of Maybe. After Women's Day she didn't even take the flask home. She gave it to the cleaner.

The manager had very often admonished her for stuffing bits of bread between the books. She said it wasn't her. She gave up her favorite hiding places for food. But she still hid bread. She got written warnings. She insisted it wasn't her. She refused to admit it. She was proud. She wore knee-length skirts made of English worsted and sheer, foreign nylons. These eccentricities of hers tired them. She was dismissed.

Benia was determined to talk to the resident who had white wavy hair.

He also had an ill-fitting denture that fell out whenever he got overexcited. Benia liked to be nearby at these moments. She'd bend down, then wheezily but gracefully pick up the false teeth. She'd toddle to the bathroom, rinse them, bring them back, and hand them to their owner.

Apparently his wife died a week before her retirement. She was a notary. She liked a tidy desk and the color turquoise. That's the color of the velvet covering the urn containing her ashes. It's standing in his room, waiting to be topped up with her husband's ashes, said Benia.

She must have had a heart of gold, chipped in Helena.

How so? wondered Benia.

I stole into his bedroom. I peeked inside the urn.

What are you saying, Helena?

Sometimes it's good to see how a person will look after all this earthly toil. You know what, Benia, it was after that talk organized for us by the company that makes urns. You remember—about the advantages of cremation over being thrown into a pit. Well, so it occurred to me that it would be a good idea to investigate in advance how and what. To be able to make a wise decision. I sneaked in with a nail file. But I opened it without needing a tool. With a fingernail. Pop. Like a coffee canister. No more than four handfuls of ash. That's all that's left of us.

You say she had a heart of gold, that wife of his.

Or nothing but gold teeth. There was a bit of metal ore inside.

Then I have no chance. No chance. My entire wealth is two hard-working hands.

But do you like him? I'm surprised, I'm very surprised. I don't like him. Though he has higher education. They say he was a qualified food engineer. He traveled all over the country. He inspected the menus at cafeterias. But you crept into his bedroom too, didn't you?

Yes, but only for a few seconds. To see the photo of his late wife. So do you want to be buried or burned?

Helena scowled. She wiped her lips with the back of her hand.

I still have time to think about it. Do I look as if I'm already off to the other world? I don't neglect myself like the other female residents. I've always been well turned out.

She glanced at Benia. She smelled of dinner. She was sitting on the edge of her chair, as in a station waiting room. With a nervous gesture she rubbed one hand against the other. They looked heavy, hard, almost black, as if full of earth. Swollen veins wound around her wrists and ran upward, disappearing under her sleeve.

And you like him, do you, Benia? asked Helena and continued:

Isn't he terribly boring? It's impossible to unwind or have fun in his company. He doesn't speak at all. And when he does, he rambles on about food and nothing else. How many calories? He talks about deep frying. And what coating they've put on the chops to make them heavier.

My late husband was the silent type too, said Benia in a mournful tone.

If that's the case, you should give it a try. If you have a taste for men like that. I'd say he's still hankering after a woman's care.

Do you really think so? asked Benia, and without waiting for a reply, went to look for the resident with white wavy hair.

He was sitting in a dressing gown tied with the belt from a woman's frock.

It's a gorgeous summer, isn't it? asked Benia, sitting down very close to him.

It's a gorgeous summer, isn't it?

She watched as his half-open mouth arched slightly. He didn't answer. He stared into space.

Can you hear me? It's a gorgeous summer, isn't it? Once, when the children had already grown up, flown the nest, I moved to the countryside, to my cousin's place. There were such beautiful lime trees in that village, you have no idea. But lime trees have to be cared for. Pruned. They can easily fall on a house. I was very keen for the storks to build a nest at our place. They strolled around the fields, you see. I made them a special place to sit on such a lovely lime tree. I can do anything around the house. Carpentry. Electricals. Even when the fridge was dripping I repaired it. I am not self-seeking where men are concerned. I don't need a handyman. For conversation, yes. More for conversation, to avoid getting bored on my own. But the storks weren't interested. And it was so nice. Made of short planks. And a little hay. A support. For the first few summers I thought maybe they couldn't see what a perfect spot it was for them. They kept flying over, but they didn't settle. Plainly they didn't want to. And then their nest with young in it was hit by lightning. After that, they never flew into the village at all. Storks have to do things their own way. My lime tree didn't appeal to them. But so what? What counts is that we're having a beautiful summer. A beautiful summer, repeated Benia louder.

What's so beautiful about it? Huh? he asked irritably, and moved, standing up and sitting down twice.

What's there to like? It's so hot people's sphincters can't hold out. Just today somebody crapped in my bed, two times. And the caregiver is trying to persuade me it was my doing. What a moron. And the doctor says it's because of bananas and tomato juice. He says that's the perfect recipe for the shits. Do you believe him?

Well, if he's a doctor, perhaps he knows what he's talking about, with regard to health, of course, said Benia, and smiled, but he went on scowling.

Everyone's got something against me, he said, standing up and sitting down.

They keep on carping at me. I'm an agreeable person. But everyone's always against me. My daughter's paying for me, after all. She's a good kid. She's in America. That's why she doesn't visit me. But she sends parcels. Food parcels. And they can't bear the fact that someone sends me something. They'd like to be getting treats from America too. I don't think they take so much care over the standards of frying in oil over there, but at least they never stint on serving large portions.

All the residents' children seem to be in America, don't they? said Benia. Suddenly she remembered something. She quivered joyfully and went on:

You know what, a hedgehog used to come see me in that village. Don't you believe me? He did, he really did. Night in, night out, he came for his meat. I made myself a little lamp in the yard so I could look at him.

A banana, what harm can an American banana do to anyone? Can you tell me that? he asked. He didn't wait for an answer, but got up, broke wind, and walked off.

Benia stayed put. She watched the residents waddling around the grass as if trying to trample it deep underground.

Truda has passed away. In her sleep, apparently, said Helena over her newspaper, drawing a mustache onto a man in a suit.

But the priest came in time with the Little Lord Jesus. He gave her the last rites, twittered Benia.

I envy those who find genuine comfort and solace in religion, grumbled Henryk, leaning his head back and covering his eyes with his fingers to stop the bright daylight from bothering him.

Caressed by the sunshine, Leokadia's face softened.

Henryk uncovered his face. He cast a furtive glance at Leokadia and said:

There's one thing to be grateful for, if only to God Himself, which is that we didn't die young. But as for old age? It's neither a gain, counting the spoils, nor a disaster. We're immune, that's what, Leokadia. Immune, he concluded, shielding himself with a hand again.

As Leokadia looked at him, Henryk seemed to go cloudy before her eyes. To become sticky and shapeless. Just a bit more and he'd turn into clotted, dirty liquid.

I was fond of our darling Truda, declared Benia.

She strongly reminded me of my momma. Just the same smoothly brushed hair. The same neat little cardigan. They both liked the color dove-gray. My dearest Truda. She treated me like her child too. She was always urging me to eat. She comforted me when I cried. She came to see me at bedtime, though she hadn't the strength anymore. She told such lovely stories about Saint Teresa. She taught me a prayer to Saint Joseph. To thee, Saint Joseph, we come in our tribulation. Our most mighty protector, bring us heavenly assistance in our struggle with the power of darkness. Amen. You say she died in her sleep, Helena. Not everyone has the luck. Not everyone. God blessed her.

The birds aren't chirping as much as at the start of the summer, have you noticed, my dears? put in Leokadia, saddened.

The bees are so languid, fully fed. It won't occur to them to sting. What an effect these heatwaves have on us all, she sighed, crumpling a handkerchief.

They say the drought's so bad the corn crops are very small. The harvest will be modest. We'll be overrun by rats again, said Miron, scratching the spot where the IV was inserted.

I lived with some dear little rats in a hole behind the fireplace. And I had nothing with me but the rosary my daddy made for me, recalled Benia.

I was around four or five years old. They didn't touch me. They never even sniffed me. But they slept close to my neck to keep me warm. It went on for three years. As soon as it got dark. They'd start to come out. I could see them through a hole, walking up and down the stairs, up and down. I won't have anything said against rats.

That's dreadful. I'm disgusted, said Henryk, making a face.

Consul, why are you so sensitive. Just think of them as great big Mickey Mice—better? hissed Miron.

Do you want to be burned or buried, do you know by now? Benia asked Leokadia, tilting her head like a puppy trying to catch high-pitched sounds.

Give it a break, said Helena, nervously leafing through the newspaper in search of another prepubescent.

You know, I think I'm dead and gone already—I'm just here to haunt you.

Henryk scowled. His face seemed incomplete, as if chipped.

A dry mattress, clean underwear, anesthetics. The complete kit for life on the brink of death. We've got everything we're likely to need.

Drawing tails onto the letters in the headlines, Helena said:

There's no alternative, my friends, one must give up the habit of living.

Miron scratched his temple. Briefly he covered his face with his hands. Then he looked at the skin on his palms, gone pink in the heat, and his forearms coated in rust-colored hairs.

They said on TV that this year people are dropping like flies. Especially the old ones who live alone.

Nobody comes to collect them from the morgue, added Bożydar.

My daughter was going to take me to the seaside. Why doesn't she come? Or call? The manager said she called, asked about my health, and told him to pass on her greetings. And that's all. Nothing to say I should pack, or that they'd be here any minute. I was supposed to be teaching my grandson to swim, said Henryk, struggling to breathe.

Hey, you old fart, you'll hold yourself up on the waves all right. The unsinkable Gammon, said Miron, patiently examining his hand. It looked bloodless.

Why can't I remember Momma's eyes? said Helena, like a spoiled child.

I can't remember her because she didn't defend me. She allowed me to be a patient beast of burden. It's strange, I have such a perfect memory of the face of the German who saved us. Light brown eyes. I can't see other faces, the house, the street, our apartment, nothing. But I can see those eyes clearly. They herded us in a flock. *Schnell* and *schnell*. Then I think someone carried me. And suddenly there he was. I can see his face, even his neck with the purple stripe from the tight collar. That sort of detail. He was so close. He drew us aside. He had a weary face. Or sad perhaps. Resigned. He told us to run away. Were we already at the station? On the platform? No, still in the town. I think Momma was forced to go farther. She didn't want to board the train. In '39, everyone was afraid they'd transport us deep inside Russia. No one thought anything worse could happen. I don't know if it's true that they shot her. She refused to get into the railcar. I can't remember. Her face. When you're only a small child, you believe things that fall apart will somehow reassemble.

Leon tore his gaze from his application for a dog. He looked at Helena.

We've been playing at nothing but burial games since childhood. We have to make do with it, he said. He went back to his writing. He formed small, shapely letters. He did his best not to write on the food stains that had marked the page.

Miron scratched his cheek. He had long fingernails, thick and grayish-yellow. He spoke quietly, unusually for him:

I'm aching from the meat at lunch. But it's all right, at least there's something to fill the time.

So what do you think about our life on the brink of death? Is it necessary to anyone? Helena asked Leon.

He sat huddled into a bare-boned chair. Frail. Fragile. In oversized pants and a coat, in spite of the heat. Sloppily shaved. Rough stubble covered his chin.

So I—

He let his head drop onto his right shoulder and fell asleep.

Why don't you ask me, Helena? I don't matter to you, complained Henryk.

Yes, you do, and how. I've always had a soft spot for lawyers. But don't think I'm going for walks with you as in the past.

I won't race along as fast. I'll adapt to your pace, Helena.

It's you who has to keep up with me, not I with you. This isn't about the fact that my legs ache. We both know that. It's about something else.

What is it now? What is it, my flame-haired temptress? he asked.

You're shamming, the whole time you never stop shamming. You hide behind amnesia, said Helena indignantly.

Dementia, dementia, cawed Miron with his eyes closed, from the depths of sleep.

Helena leaned toward Henryk, as if in great confidence. As if in a whisper:

You expose yourself, my dear.

I do?

You parade along the passage with your wiener on show, pretending to be in search of the bathroom. I don't like it. I don't like that in men. I am a lady, and I insist that a man should behave like a gentleman.

He walks about with his pee-pee on offer. Maybe one of the ladies will be tempted, screeched Miron.

I wanted to ask you the way to the bathroom, said Henryk to excuse himself.

No, my dear Consul, you wanted to show it to me.

But Helena. I had no clean pajama bottoms. I couldn't ask the caregivers two nights running. They say the washerwoman has gone on holiday.

Not only are you an exhibitionist, you're a liar too. You wanted to show it. I know that perfectly well. I can assure you I haven't forgotten what it looks like yet. And you're not going to refresh my memory.

Yesterday he was standing in the roses with his pecker on display too, said Miron, contemplating the finger he'd removed from his ear.

Because I wasn't going to reach the toilet in time, explained Henryk.

That'll be the day. So who's going to extract the thorns from your pecker? laughed Miron, wheezing.

I wasn't going to make it in time, can't you see? I wasn't going to be in time. You folks are mean, sobbed Henryk.

Cringing, he went off to his room, in tears. Wobbling like a new-born foal.

My little boy was just as cute and pink, puffed Benia.

I'm told he's gone bald, you know, that son of mine. And he had hair like a girlie. In the labor ward already. The nurses tied a bow on him. Like a doll. A chubby little face with such sweet curls. He's sure to come tomorrow.

Never mind if he doesn't visit. As long as he does the burying, said Leokadia.

Good God, whined Benia. She had nothing in her mouth, but her face looked as if she were chewing constantly, indifferent and weary.

Helena was contemplating the idea that out there on the other side of the fence people were forming plans, working, making calls. Buying fruit bursting with juice. Women were trying on outfits, men were watching them with drowsy desire. They were changing the bouquets in vases. Making love during the siesta, with the blinds down, keeping in the scent of lovers. They were packing bags and suitcases. Calling out to children. Setting off on vacation. Car horns were heralding the start of a journey. The beaches were filling up. The whole world was squirming from the din of holidaymakers.

Here, behind the closed gate, it was quiet, as the science of sparing one's gestures, stinting on words, and withholding glances was practiced. Everything was bursting from the heat. Rampant. Proliferating. Pushing people into the background. Beyond the mercy of nature.

Leokadia and Henryk spent the entire afternoon watching one of the men with a purple growth on his temple. He'd laugh. Then instantly become sad. Minutes later, he'd laugh again. Loudly. For no reason. Or at his own thoughts. Then he'd sink into torpor again, punctuated by hoarse cackling.

I used to talk to him a lot. But then it was as if someone had cut him off with a knife—he stopped talking, and does nothing but that, said Henryk at a certain point.

He was quiet for ages. But, permanently wide open, his mouth continued to take in the fresh air.

Leokadia nodded.

She noticed that Henryk's eyes were disappearing. The sockets were filling with gluey gunk.

And our Benia fell off the toilet seat, said Leokadia. Her busy little lips curved into a mournful grimace.

She was afraid to drink. She couldn't swallow. Because she was wetting herself more and more often, and we know what the caregivers are like. They'll report it right away and send her to the house by the lake. So our Benia was getting dehydrated. I did notice something, she had rings around her eyes and sunken cheeks. She sat on the toilet seat in the evening, and fell off it during the night. They found her this morning. She's on a drip. They might do a gastroscopy. She must have felt dizzy, don't you think?

The reason she couldn't drink wasn't because she was losing control, *excusez-moi*. But because she had a hiatus hernia. But that's a very trivial complaint. She couldn't bend over, that's all. I have a more exotic illness. I brought it back from Africa, proclaimed Henryk.

And do you know what the manager has introduced? A toilet paper dispenser for the one-handed. But my sister wasn't at all impressed. I'm so pleased whenever the manager thinks of us.

As soon as I arrived here I noticed that it's a professionally equipped home. Ramps instead of steps. Raised toilet bowls. Handles. Rails. Electric sockets at waist height. It all helps a person to forget he's suffering from an extremely uncommon ailment.

What about the bedpans? And the urinals, Consul? What I like best are the meals on wheels. They bring them to my room. They leave me alone. Then come to fetch the plates.

The ones they take food to are on the way out already. Any day now they're off to the house by the lake.

What are you saying?

If nobody supervises them, they don't eat anything. And the caregivers are just itching to scrape the food off their plates into a plastic bag and take it home for their piglets. Haven't you noticed? Our caregivers don't look like city folks.

But if they don't supervise, one can self-regulate how much one wants to eat.

That's not self-regulation, it's creative euthanasia. You must eat with us, on the terrace. If you don't, you won't be necessary to anyone. Thin means sick. And sick means needing more looking after. I know what it is to be unnecessary. I've been unnecessary all my life. First at the shelter, because I cried. Grandma put a pillow over my face to keep me quiet. That's how I learned to hold my breath. I very rarely inhaled. I was only all right in the chimney vent. I felt quite at home in there. And in the arms of a certain woman. But never mind about that.

And I left my lymph nodes in the camp, announced Leokadia.

At the orphanage I was in bandages. Like a rag doll. I was afraid to walk. Helena said I screamed terribly with every step. I can't remember a thing. Strange. I should do, I'm the older. There were a lot of children like us in that place. In the orphanage. Boys and girls. They called our room Loonyville. There were three- or four-story bunkbeds in there. Like at the camp. Everyone wanted to sleep on top. Because if you slept lower down, lice fell on your face all night long. Only afterward, years later, when someone finally came up with the idea of sending me to an optician, did I turn out to have really bad eyesight. And I must have suffered from monstrous headaches. Helena always took care of me. But I didn't like her husband. Someone told us he'd been in the ghetto. He stood by the gate. I don't know if that's true. If he really did work for the Germans. She probably didn't know about it. She couldn't have known. I wouldn't have given him the time of day, but there were so few of us left. Those of us who hadn't left the country had to stick together. Maybe that's why she thought he was so wonderful.

Leokadia took her foot out of her slipper.

Henryk had never seen such a white foot. Petite, arched. A network of fine veins, like a blue cobweb, shone through the skin. Only the toes were a normal flesh color. Probably from the pressure of her shoes.

But he died. Helena's a widow. Let him simply remain dead. Let the dead be at peace.

Leokadia fell silent.

She watched as a woman on the next deck chair hypnotized herself by swinging a Virgin Mary medallion to and fro on her finger. It swayed with the docile movement of a pendulum. Another female resident, despite the heat, was wrapped in a coat with a red fur collar. Her face was tight, alert, marked by pain and resignation. It was the look of a vixen caught in a rusty trap.

I wouldn't want Benia to pass on. It would be boring.

Leokadia, what sort of problems are these? What about the war, the last one? And before that, the Polish-Bolshevik war? And the May Coup? The Uprising? And you're sorry for Benia. What about martial law? Aren't you sorry the string trio isn't coming? Last year they were here by now.

Is your room warm at night?

I don't know, I take a tablet and sleep like a baby.

My husband used to walk around at night. He liked to eat. I can see him now. Rummaging in the fridge. The little light under the freezer compartment used to brush against his bald patch like a parrot feather.

I had a voracious woman in my life. And as at table, so in bed. That's how I'd define her temperament. She had an unusual body. Bony. Lenten. Not a trace of fat. No graceful curves on her hips or thighs. Her gluttony was hidden. Only practiced at home. In secret. You understand.

Mine was thin too, but he liked to appease his hunger. Afterward he'd suffer from bellyache, flatulence, heartburn, stomach spasms, diarrhea, and acid reflux. But he said it was from grief, not overeating. From profound grief, which dilutes the gastric juices and impairs intestinal peristalsis.

What can one do? Some people are born into families full of suicides and auto-cannibals. Which in any case comes to the same thing. She killed herself. That bony woman of mine. She was like a ravenous bitch. She could eat the whole time. Choke, bring it up, empty her bowels, and go on eating. She ate fast. In a hurry. She didn't grind it up. She swallowed large chunks. She wouldn't waste time smacking her lips. Or chewing. Indulging her palate. She gulped it down. Stuffed herself. She was happy to eat standing up. In the kitchen. She fed at night too. She'd sit at the table. Stand in the pantry. By the fridge. Leaning against the cupboard. She'd gorge with her eyes shut. As if not awake. She'd eat while sleeping.

Was she your wife?

He shuddered when she asked him this question.

He confirmed with a nod.

The radiators in my room are cold. I freeze.

It's lucky there's hot water. Though one shampoo for ten is too little. Unless you're Miron. So what about the trio—will they come, Leokadia? Do you still believe that?

Yes, yes, they'll come. They're sure to be on their way already. Just look how those sparrows like to amuse themselves. They act very oddly. Watch the way they fly up, then wait for them to drop the moment a breeze sets the air in motion.

The summer became pure light, burning hot, giving no respite. The residents were moving away from themselves. Becoming divisible. Split apart. Their bodies seemed to be dwindling by the day. Sinking in the garden furniture, getting mired in their deck chairs.

On the forecourt, among the close-cut grass, daisies had seeded themselves. They looked like scattered pink buttons.

Some of the female residents took particular pleasure in picking the flowers and then sticking them back in the ground. This occupied them for hours on end. Until the caregivers chased them away.

Most of them held a crumpled handkerchief. The staff made sure it wasn't paper. Easily swallowed. In danger of sticking to lips, dentures, or wet noses. Cotton ones were best. Clutching them brought relief. Perfect for wiping the corners of the mouth, watery eyes, and sweaty palms. Something to hold onto at bad moments.

Sprinklers sliced the air with streams of water. It was almost humming. The lawn was bursting with moisture. Surging in a green wave. Soft and boggy.

Benia remembered the walks she took with her children. When they were still little. Just a few years old. They ran around barefoot. They'd slide across the wet lawn, and the little mongrel Perełka would drink straight from the hydrant, disrupting the stream of water with her hairy muzzle.

Helena kept her distance. Since Truda had gone, the Little Nightingale had filled her place. Not long ago, she couldn't have conceived that the Little Nightingale had survived. She could still see her in the pit of corpses. With a face that floated up, dripping, a foot in a twisted little boot, and hair stuck to her rain-drenched skull.

But now, day after day, she imagined that they'd emerged from behind the wire together. The Little Nightingale and she, inseparable as ever, first in line for blood samples, for swallowing medicine, for being photographed. There they stand, with the ramp in the background, holding hands. The British snap picture after picture. And then, on request, the Little Nightingale rolls up her striped uniform, pulls back the sleeve, and shows the number. But Helena hasn't the strength to bend over, and the Little Nightingale helps to pull up her pant leg so they can see the tattoo on her thigh.

As Helena went for her walks, she fantasized that the Little Nightingale had had more luck. Her talent had attracted adoptive parents to the orphanage. She'd settled in Vienna, and invited her to her concerts; they'd gone shopping, they'd bought sweaters, then gone for coffee. Forcibly forgotten ever since, now the Little Nightingale was with her all the time. Day after day. Night after night. As when they used to huddle together, listening out for Dr. Josef's footsteps.

The heat wave softened the world, making it smudged and sticky.

Time seemed extendible, still and heavy. The high temperature sealed every second like wax.

Leokadia liked to talk about her husband. She only did it in the sole presence of Mr. Krawiecki. Deaf. Taciturn. He basked in the warmth of other people's words, without even knowing it. He'd sit with her on a bench beside the rose bushes. He'd offer his gnarled, swollen hands to the sunshine and hide his face in a scarf.

Leokadia always began with the slipper. In her soft, childish voice she'd say she was preparing a name-day party when she found her husband's slipper in the freezer compartment, lying between a frost-coated duck and the ice cubes.

But two years later she started finding his reading glasses in the fridge. A burned-out lightbulb. A bundle of rubber bands for jam-jar tops, which for some unknown reason he'd started to collect. At this point a comb was no longer a comb for him, it had lost its name, it was "that thing for your hair." Had she seen that thing for . . . You know—for doing your hair, for combing, he'd keep asking, stroking the back of his head with an open palm. He was drifting away from her, drifting away from himself too.

One day, looking out of the kitchen window, she noticed her husband circling their building several times. Slowly. Reverently. He revealed his nervous state by constantly throwing back his fine, thinning hair. He examined the texture of the façade, the window frames on the ground floor and the metal carpet-beating frame. He'd go closer, stop, take a good look, stare, and feel with his hand. With the curiosity of first sight.

It took her a while to realize that he wasn't out for a walk, he wasn't exploring, studying or inspecting, but trying to go home, to get inside, but he'd forgotten where the entrance was.

She went downstairs. He was calm, submissive, suddenly mindless. He let himself be led by the hand, straight to the door of their apartment; now and then he smiled and turned his head to look into her face. She was sure he didn't know who she was.

In time she stopped talking to him. She only said what was necessary, essential, practical. Later on she said nothing.

But his body had started to desire her again, like long ago, when he'd spotted her in the tram one summer afternoon. She was in a bright yellow shirtdress and a Basque beret, slightly covering an eye. She was standing by the middle entrance, holding the overhead rail. The inky number was protruding from under her sleeve. Then, she was sure, he gained courage, and liked her brown hair more and more. Locks the color of dark chocolate. Curled into thick cords. Falling onto her breast, onto the spheres lifted by her bra, and which fitted so easily in his open palms.

He followed her down one of those small streets in Żoliborz, a woman as slender as the saplings planted along the sidewalk by the local community.

She could feel his presence too, coming closer and closer.

Forty-six years on, he didn't know what the vacuum cleaner was for, and the shower terrified him. She wrote instructions in block letters on every object in the apartment, its name and what it was for.

It's on the tip of my tongue, he kept saying, in search of words. Scratched. Bruised. He kept falling over. He kept forgetting the layout of the apartment. He'd crash into the furniture. The walls. At night he wanted to go to church, to the store, he'd dress for bed in gloves and scarf.

He went on hitting her. And she gave it back. More and more

often, but more feebly, with less of a swing, the way some people scold a naughty child, but even so he was frightened, fearful. Like a dog you chase off by throwing a slipper. He'd toddle forward, then go round and round in circles until he found his bedroom. He'd put his legs into the sleeves of his shirt as if it were a pair of pants. Or sit in an armchair. Run his fingers along those rubber bands, for hours on end.

When he died, she sat down in that armchair of his; the fabric was soiled, worn through, it smelled of urine. She hadn't the strength to weep, or to move from the armchair, for several days.

After the funeral she went down into the cellar. They used to come here together. At one time, in the past, when he was in his prime, when he liked the bottle. He'd make her sit on a lumpy couch amid dusty jars, bottles, and chipped flower pots. He'd kneel down before a demijohn and drink sour, failed apple wine through a tube. Now and then he'd get up, chortle, rub his hands, kneel down again, and form his lips into a spout. She would watch him, her mind on something else. She'd sit opposite, he wanted her to be there. Once he was drunk, he'd move around on all fours, groping for the cardboard suitcase in which he kept his striped uniform from the camp. He'd put the worn-out, ragged garment on her. He'd order her to stand to attention. To count. *Ein, zwei, drei.* In various voices. As if she weren't standing alone before him, but as if there were lots and lots of her. He'd bark instructions. Prod her. Order her to report what had happened to her today. It was never good enough. Either she was slouching. Talking too softly. Out of step. He'd hit her. Push her. Out of anger. Out of fear. He'd come up from behind and pinch her neck. Pull her hair. Stick his fingers between her buttocks.

Despite the pain she willingly submitted to these drills. She had never seen him as happy as in those threadbare striped pajamas. She understood him, he wasn't longing for the camp, he was missing childhood, even one spent amid lice, nits, and on all fours.

He'd keep saying: A child is like a dog, it can get used to anything.

Finally, when he'd finished his performance, he'd cry. He'd lie on the concrete, on his back, not moving. He'd drift away. Mired in memories.

Toward the end of his life he'd stopped drinking. He'd stand in the window and smoke. Hour after hour. Staring at who knows what. He'd light one cigarette off the last.

He'd never had it easy. He was eleven when the war ended. He'd found an aunt. For several years he'd helped her husband to sell herring at the market. But when he married, they didn't give him a single chair to call his own. Not even a hug for the start of his new life. They had nothing to offer him. As if he were a stranger. Not theirs.

When he died, Leokadia covered him with a quilt. With just his small, birdlike head protruding. A look of astonishment—as if his own death had surprised him, come at the wrong time.

Afternoon tea was over.

Blancmange. Once again they'd served vanilla blancmange with a splash of jam. Most of the residents didn't move from the table, in expectation of cherries. Each was looking forward to their favorite kind: large with thin skin, small, sweet, watery. Stringy, tart, like sour cherries. Or light, white or also dark, purple, fleshy, almost mealy. Pretty, compact, a pity to eat them. Shapeless, pecked by starlings, gone bad, too moldy to eat, like a bitter, watery bladder. With tiny stones, flimsy peel. Or else huge, hard, well-padded with pulp, enveloping all the sweetness.

Henryk savored the memory of the mangoes he'd eaten in Africa. He'd describe the thick, sickly-sweet juice slowly trickling down his chin.

But they always shouted him down: Cherries, our cherries. Each person wanted to tell about the ones they'd had in childhood. The men boasted of the high trees they'd climbed. Quickly. Barefoot. Knees hugging a rebellious trunk. How they'd picked the fruits from the very top, while the branches shook, bending to the ground. The women fondly remembered twin cherries. They'd hooked them on their ears. Worn them with pride, like ruby earrings. They wouldn't let each other speak.

Each one wanted to be heard. Once, long ago, they had eaten the best, the most wonderful cherries. From Grandma's basket. From Grandpa's rough hands. From Momma's lips. From Father. From a lover. A fiancé. A newly married wife. A stranger.

They were looking forward to their cherries.

Benia was picking up breadcrumbs. Moving around on all fours. Patiently roving under the tables, one at a time.

Miron was clinging to the back of his chair. He looked bloodless. Sallow. Sullen. Well past his best. Sweaty strands of hair stuck to his brow. Large drops of perspiration glistened. He was watching a resident who had been going up and down the step into the garden for the past fifteen minutes.

What an old fart our Consul has become. He's aged over the summer. Face covered in blotches. Skull all over scabs. Crawling with blemishes. They could at least put bandages on him. Am I supposed to look at that while eating? For what sins. His hands shake. His pajamas stink from way off. Have you seen his diapers poking through the fly? Just take a look. I'd rather buy the farm than be among people in that state. The Consul. What sort of a diplomat can he have been? He can't even negotiate a few cherries.

That's not Henryk. Henryk is sitting here. Right here, he's asleep next to you. That man is from room eight, or . . . From the room next to the office, explained Leokadia patiently. She was upset. She'd forgotten to ask for a panty liner. Now it was too late. She was afraid, watching the caregiver tanning herself on a deck chair—that one had it in for those who soiled themselves. She kept a special notebook, wrote down the names of anyone incontinent, anyone with loose bowels, and never overlooked a candidate for the house by the lake.

But I recognize him. Henryk, said Miron indignantly. He spat through his teeth. His face seemed to be putrefying in the heat.

That's Henryk. Gammon. Our Consul. I'm telling you. He bowed to me, didn't he.

The man from number eight bows to everyone. Just in case. He knows he has amnesia, and he doesn't want to offend anyone, Leokadia made clear, without taking her eyes off the caregiver.

What do you mean amnesia, you've forgotten what amnesia is. He's got dementia. Dementia, clucked Miron.

But immediately stopped talking. Into the dining room came the manager.

Ladies and gentlemen, would you please stop sending me requests for cherries. It's out of the question. I'm rejecting all of them. Every single one. Hush over there. Please don't whisper. Now I can see some of you are just pretending to be deaf. But as soon as something's up, you can hear it all. And now I'll tell you the rationalization. Just one single time.

Helena could see the inside of his mouth. Purple. Almost black, as if he'd been eating blueberries or warty blackberries. Or like the palate of a puppy pulled from a sack by the scruff of its neck. Jaws forced apart to show a hesitant buyer, with assurances that with this sooty interior it'll bloody well bark fiercely.

Please don't invade my office, repeated the manager.

I shan't explain again. You all want to live as long as possible, right? And we, the entire staff, want the same. But I wish you would please remember that last year two of the residents choked on cherry pits, and Gabriela, or whatever she's called, is still in a coma after a pit got stuck in her windpipe. Enough said. That's all for now. Thank you for your attention. *Bon appétit*. Ah, one more thing: the priest is coming today. If anyone has the desire or a heavy heart.

Or a soiled conscience? added the caregiver with a laugh.

Leokadia noticed that she was missing a few teeth. She looked like the pumpkin they'd put in the common room on All Souls Day, to try to be American. This pumpkin mouth had made it impossible for Leokadia to swallow anything at all.

Poor priest. He wants to convert us. I'm sorry for him, said Helena, scratching her earlobe, red from a mosquito bite.

Well, I shall take communion. I like our priest. He listens. He gives advice. Where to go. What plans to make for the life eternal, moaned Benia, emerging from under the table.

Yesterday the priest complained about the staff, said Helena in a soft tone.

The caregiver mixed up the rooms. He gave last rites to the wrong patient, so someone's going to hell, not to the right-hand side.

She looked at the head of Benia, sitting at her feet. Her hair was visibly thinning. Her grimy ears were covered in little scabs.

Miron bent over, groaning. He was trying to cut holes in his sneakers with a pair of scissors. He struggled away, sticking out his tongue for assistance. The tip of the scissors stubbornly jabbed at the material.

But what a lovely smile our priest has. And he gets bored so quickly. He gives you absolution in the middle of your confession.

Benia nodded several times in a gesture of mock salutation.

When I think about God, I feel like a mouse being toyed with by a tomcat. I envy anyone who believes their soul will fly off to heaven, replied Helena.

I married a kindhearted, decent, and very boring woman. May the earth rest lightly upon her. I am sure my wife has a wonderful life beyond the grave. But not a coeducational one, I hope. More like a sort of amusement park for kids, said Miron, and laughed, not as he wanted to—with all his strength. The cackling brought on a prolonged fit of coughing. He threw down the shoe and the scissors, which fell under the table.

The priest may be a bad priest, but what a good father he is. He has educated his two children. And to be doctors, laughed Miron.

I don't believe those mean rumors spread by the antichrists swarming around here. I don't believe it, period. It's the manager who puts it around. He's mad because we get along well with the priest, said Benia indignantly, running her fingers through the hair on her temples.

I was joking, said Miron, laughing. The priest brought me a magazine about airplanes.

The nurses began to bring round trays with drugs and little glasses of water.

I'm in favor of the priest too, nodded Benia. They say our

parish is modest. But at the one near the station they're always building something. Apparently they bought a large crucifix with a backlit Jesus. Each nail is a little light. Our parish priest is poor. He's a real priest, but the other one has a graveyard. He has the money to pay for the light, she explained, spat on her hand, then smoothed her bangs with it. I wonder if the priest wants to be burned or buried, she speculated, closing her eyes to concentrate.

But one must admit that for him we aren't Nobodies. He can see us, and that's now, when to almost everyone we're invisible, said Helena.

Wanting to say more, she opened her mouth, but gave up—interrupted, from across the lawn, by the raised voice of a nurse. She was coming from the direction of the gate. For the second shift, not wearing her tunic yet, but in an off-the-shoulder summer dress.

She jabbered away: I'm amazed, personally I'm quite amazed you ladies and gentlemen can eat your dinner in such a stench. You can smell it out in the street, out in the city, you can tell someone's pooped his pants. It's sure to be our dear engineer Leon. You say you want a dog, but you won't make the effort to go on a short walk.

Leon got up, wobbling, finding it hard to stand upright. He wanted to speak like a Roman orator, but choked and spluttered, almost in tears:

My parents would never have put me in here.

Oh yeah, your momma's gonna roll in her grave three times over when she sees what happens to naughty old boys who crap themselves.

Gradually it was getting dark.

Can you smell the sea? asked Henryk, staring into space.

Nobody answered.

I can always scent out the sea. Always. Even from several kilometers away. The rich air. The marvelous breeze. The iodine, he said with relish, licking his lips.

Helena didn't want to go back to her room. She didn't like lying in bed. She hadn't slept properly since the camp. At best, shallow sleep that didn't give respite. She just dozed. If not for the caregivers' nagging, she'd spend all night on the terrace. She knew it was time to go to her room. The pictures in the newspaper were becoming blurred. She could feel the cold, a chill in her legs that seemed inexplicable. After all, it was still very hot. The day was ending, but the air refused to cool down.

How fucked-up this life is. Fucked-up, Miron agreed with himself.

How can you say that? It's beautiful. Simply beautiful. Sweet as honey. Like the taste of candy. You just have to know how to savor it, replied Helena through tight lips.

It's fucked-up. This life is fucked-up. It used to be all right. Remember? We slept in the snow. Barefoot. In torn rags. We didn't even catch cold, Helena, and how.

I never slept in the snow with you, dear Miron.

What do you mean? But we ran away together. They chased us right across town, said Miron, sitting up in his deck chair and squinting at Helena.

I admit it, they chased me too, but across a different town, she explained, without looking at him.

Try to remember. We fed on roots, your hand got messed up. It had to be taken off, and then, he said, trying to remind her, but finally waved a hand to admit defeat.

You're right, what's the point of reminiscing. You or someone else, she whispered, closed her eyes, and sank torpidly into the deck chair.

I always despise myself after lunch. I eat too much. One shouldn't stuff oneself. It's enough to be alive, confessed Leokadia.

It was supper last, not lunch, Benia corrected her. But the suppers are good for nothing too. Right, Leolka? In the past, after supper you'd bathe the kids, chase them off to bed and have the perfect evening. Just me and my husband. He'd tell me what was going on at work, and I'd make tomorrow's dinner, she said, polishing the table top with her sleeve.

The suppers are like any other. But the breakfasts, simply awful. Everything minced up, huffed Henryk, ineptly masking his satisfaction with anger. As he always did when the conversation came around to his favorite topic. This isn't a refuge for penniless old folks. Everyone has dentures here. And as for the helpings. Like for birds. When I was in Africa, I knew where I got my vim. An antelope haunch on the fire. Rare, juicy, super fresh. But here.

It's true that the food here is not one of the assets of the place. No wonder we trail along close to the walls. We haven't the strength to walk. Just one step, and I feel as if I've been slogging away for a whole year, said Helena. And they try to persuade us it's osteoporosis to blame. For lack of calcium. That our bones are like sponge. But they'd only have to serve us a little normal food. If you eat, you look good. If you look good, you're healthy. And if you're healthy, you stay alive. I've always made sure my face is nicely made-up, with a rosy complexion.

I could make you a great poppyseed cake. With full-fat, buttery poppyseed. Finger-licking good. I know where to buy that kind, said Benia, smoothing her eyebrows with a saliva-coated finger.

French croissants. Buttery. Light as a puff of Parisian air on a blazing hot day in Montmartre, mused Henryk. Or little tartlets from exotic seas. Warmed up. Filled with cherries fished out of compote. Or hot apple pie coated in sour cream. Buttered lobster. Scrumptious, he said, smacking his lips and straining his eyes, in an effort to dig the dish out of his memory, once again see it, taste it for real, not just in his memory. Restlessly he moistened his lips, looking as if any moment now his bulging eyeballs would pop out for joy.

Rare steaks in a thick crust of salt, offered Helena, and Benia added: Vegetable salad. Just right for Saint Szczepan's and Saint John's day. All chopped the same size. Diced small. Fresh cucumber. Pickled gherkin. A little parsley. A bit of apple. A carrot. A hard-boiled egg. Homemade mayonnaise. It never gave anyone wind.

Guinea fowl in horseradish sauce, said Helena, suddenly laughing, with a stifled cackle, as if her mouth were gagged.

Slurping, Henryk continued: My daughter used to make the most exquisite goose liver pâté. Every Sunday I used to buy good wine for my son-in-law. And a bunch of flowers for my daughter. Candy for my granddaughter. I know what I'm talking about: goose liver pâté with a French red.

There was a hotel in Wrocław, near the station, where they served the best herrings with vodka, said Miron, opening his eyes. Cold slices under a coat of beets. No flies on that. What a great snack. You'd drink all night without a hangover. Or pork in aspic with a double shot. It made your face screw up.

Suddenly his mouth, nose and eyes changed into a wrinkled ball.

Benia clapped: A great big bowl. With lots of hazelnuts in it. And a scattering of walnuts. The kids used to eat them by the handful. They'd pick out the raisins, all stuck together. They'd be pleased because they didn't know they were in there. Right at the bottom. I got two packets of raisins from the woman next door. They were sent to her in a parcel from Canada.

Miron wiped his mouth with the back of his hand. He sat more comfortably on his deck chair. He was gearing up for a major speech. He swallowed his saliva. He took in a breath of air: Potato soup made with oatmeal. I can still taste it on my lips. My mom's potato soup made with oatmeal. The best on earth. So what would you big shots say to rye dried on the stove. After the war the poverty was acute. We ground the rye with stones. Put it in a big pot. Covered it with snow, straight from the yard. You only had to heat it up a bit. It was good. Really good. You could keep chewing it forever. What you prized most was what you could keep in your mouth the longest. My older brother, Tobiasz, didn't make it through to the end of the war. He used to wander the fields, poking around in the furrows. He had a flair for picking up some kind of tuber. What was it? Hell knows. But it sure was good. Sweet. Like some fancy foreign thing. He knew the forest, that brother of mine. Three whole winters we sat in a mound. And he was just a kid, but he used to sneak out. He always brought something back, said Miron, huddling up. He was breathing heavily, rapidly, like a rabbit hit by pellets.

He was killed by shrapnel. I have marks on my chin. It ripped his belly apart. But this life is so fucked-up. So fucked-up, he whined.

How can you say that, Miron? Life is beautiful. It's simply beautiful. Like a piece of candy in the mouth, Leokadia corrected him.

Did you folks hear? Apparently the hooligans painted the wall on the street side. The manager was mad, said Henryk, sharing the news.

Without ceasing to rub the table top, Benia confirmed it: Yes, yes. The lowlifes. They wrote: Do what you like. Screw you. Fancy writing that! Do what you like. They have no respect for old people. They don't care about them.

Those scumbags don't even go away on vacation like decent people. Vandals. They should be socialized. Or penalized, said Henryk with a whistle.

They're poets, not hooligans, Helena defined them. When I ran away, I saw plenty of that. Especially when traveling by train.

Bożydar raised his head from his notebook and confirmed: Hooligans. I used to chase them around the housing project. They scrawled on my garage: Your vagina barks at me every night.

He leaned forward again, counting up the votes for his petition not to shut the television room at night.

If it's poetry, better leave it there. There's no need to paint over it, decided Leokadia. And added:

I think a good sonnet can guide us through the blackest night of our lives. What a romantic. A real little lady, laughed Miron. The cackle brought on coughing.

Honest people don't write silly little poems, declared Szymon, sitting down in a chair. They just communicate directly. As for example in accountancy. Debit—credit. Without all those metaphors, he scowled, doing up a coat button. His breathing was slow.

It may be a lovely summer, but you can never be sure. You never know with the rain. You never know, said Benia, licking her lips. Checking with the tip of her tongue to see if the sores were still there.

Bożydar sat up straight. We'll pull off a victory, he announced. I've made a precise count. We have eighty percent support. They can't shut the common room. I shall personally ensure that everyone can watch the TV at night.

He went up to Helena: Have you ever seen a cloud factory?

The reek from his mouth pushed her away from him.

Drawing out his syllables, he whispered dreamily: A machine for making clouds. It's in the mountains. In the valleys. After the rain, water steams from the gullies. It twists, it turns, it kicks. And out jumps a cloud. I'll show it to you. I promise. But now I'm off on a solitary stroll, he concluded loudly, then hunched up, and started walking toward the building.

I get the impression that for some time now our Bożydar has

been having trouble with his prostate, his bladder, his rectum, diagnosed Henryk, then became pensive.

Do you folks want to hear about the mountains? asked Miron.

They didn't reply. No one so much as nodded.

Henryk cracked his knuckles. He stared at Benia's hair, slick with sweat.

Well then, listen up, began Miron. Little bubbles of saliva were bursting on his lips. Are you listening, for fuck's sake, or not? he said, wriggling and squirming, as every movement caused him pain.

My one and only son went out of the house and didn't return. He never came back. He loved the mountains so much. When he wasn't married yet, we used to do a lot of hiking in the mountains. Just him and me. He preferred to go climbing with his dad than with his pals. He was a good boy.

You've never told us about him, interrupted Helena.

Yes, I have, I have told you. But nobody listens to anyone here. Everyone just gabbles to themselves. I once told you he works in Boston. I said he's an engineer at a glider factory. I was somewhat deviating from the truth, as they say. He never went to America. He was thirty-two when he left the house and never came back. But he used to make model gliders. I even have some of them here. They're in my bedroom. I gave one to one of the caregivers for her little boy. These days they don't have that kind in the stores. He left the house and didn't return. All my life I searched for him. He was a man of few words. Secretive. Not like me, as if he weren't my son. Just his eyes were the same. Like a wolf's. A woman once told me I have the eyes of a wolf, he said, then suddenly broke off and became pensive. He let his head droop. It looked as if he were dozing.

For my fortieth birthday my husband gave me a Rosenthal plate with a little wolf on it, said Helena. A cream-colored plate with a gold rim. When it broke, I cried as if for a child. It's shameful to admit it, my dears, truly shameful. Fancy sobbing over some pieces of broken china. As if for a child.

Miron raised his head.

Helena was watching him closely. He had such blue eyes. As she looked at them, she could feel it calming her down. It occurred to her that eyes like those never looked old. She wished she had irises like that too.

Are you listening about my son or not? he said angrily. You talk about broken plates, ladybugs, kicking the bucket, on and on the same. But my son went out and never came back. They showed his picture on the TV four times. But it was no good. He went out and didn't return. Like a stone down a well, said Miron, taking a deep breath. He looked as if breathing caused him pain. I wanted to bury him. At least bury him. But the way it's gonna be, he won't bury me, nor I him. I was told it was stress that made him like that. He built his own house. He calculated the dimensions himself, and he built it after work with his own hands. He was very skilled, at making models and houses too. My daughter-in-law said he used to shout in his sleep. He beat himself up worrying that he'd positioned the rebar badly, and the ceiling would come crashing down on them. They had three small children. All girls. After that he couldn't sleep. And he left. He never even called to say he was alive. Never wrote a letter.

Perhaps he still will, Miron, dear. You must pray. Say the rosary, Benia consoled him, rubbing her hands against her skirt at thigh level.

Perhaps. Perhaps. As long as you're alive there can always be a perhaps, he agreed, wheezing noisily.

He's sure to write, declared Leokadia.

Szymon was fidgeting in his chair. I'll tell you something. Ever since this summer has been strutting its stuff, and Leokadia's been so thrilled with it, I've had just one thought going around in my head. He paused for a moment, as if wanting to bring the insistent idea closer. I washed my mother, right? I washed my dead mother. An hour after her demise, he said and broke off. He ran his gaze over the assembled company. I dressed her. Right? With my own hands. I picked her up and laid her in the coffin. Right. All out of love. All of it, out of love. She was so brightened up. But what about me? What about us, you may have thought.

He paused. He swallowed saliva. Some lush from the Kiss of Eden funeral home will jerk us around. Apparently the manager's brother owns the place. The maximum processing suits him fine. So what do you say to that, you clever suckers?

Give it a break with all the gab about dying, said Miron, waving a hand. Wham-bam, and it's all over. Like for dogs.

Hushaby, hush, prescribed Benia sleepily. Off to your eternal rest.

I don't know what it'll be like to die. I don't know. But death is already beside us, said Leokadia, adjusting her wig. She glanced at her sister, who was sitting in her chair, leaning back. Her eyes were closed. She looked like the doll Leokadia had gotten from Santa Claus at the orphanage. Dug out of the rubble in the town. Plastic. Damaged. With bulging eyes. Hard. Impossible to cuddle. It wasn't just cheap trash, made of rags. That's what the Mother Superior told her, in her red cap and stuck-on cotton-wool beard. When Leokadia tilted the doll, it closed its eyes. After she'd played with it for a few days, one of the eyelids fell off, and the doll only winked with its left eye. It did so to this day. Trapped in her bedroom. In plastic wrap, behind a row of pictures and the wooden head—a stand for her wig. Each night, as Leokadia struggled to take her skirt off, the doll would look at her. Its heart in plastic, like in formalin, remained loving for all eternity.

Benia shook off her lethargy. She stood up. Bowed. Sat down and said: I didn't even know my children had applied for them to take me in here. I couldn't believe it, she complained, as an unhealthy flush flooded her face. Right to the end, I couldn't believe it. Even when they did my packing. I sat on the couch and said nothing. I didn't answer those questions: Did I want this, or that, what wouldn't I need anymore. They were so sad. My daughter was sobbing like mad. Maybe that's why I couldn't believe it. To the very end I couldn't believe it. Even when they brought me here. When they told us to sit downstairs in the hall and wait for the manager to register me. Even then I couldn't believe it, said Benia, shaking her head, and running her semi-conscious, glassy gaze over the residents. Of the entire house I only took what could be carried out in two hands. Like in the Uprising. Nothing more. Just what I needed, and she fell silent.

Truda talked sense, said Miron.

Ow, it got me, moaned Henryk, clutching his ribs.

Benia kept tugging at her clothes. Tidying. Gathering, stretching, and smoothing the material.

I wonder who bought my dressing table? mused Helena. I forgot to ask the antique dealer. I heard it was gone in a week. I loved doing my make-up at that table. It was lovely. So capacious.

You had so many cosmetics, but you could put them away in all those drawers, compartments and recesses. There were so many. And crystal flasks too. And those French pom-pom key rings. And the caskets. Little velvet boxes. Each one lovelier than the next. And the lacquer chest. Red lacquer with black flamingoes, recalled Leokadia. She looked at Benia. She'd grown thinner. Much thinner. Every Sunday she took communion. She was lighter than the Host.

I still have lots of cosmetics. You have to look nice. You must always be pretty, stressed Helena.

When are they finally going to give us cherries, complained Miron. His face stretched in a scowl.

If only I could make you morello cherry jam. I only picked the overripe cherries. Wine red. Fat and juicy inside. So fleshy. The pits came out easily, just using my fingers. I wish you could taste it. My children could eat it all year round. Every day of the week. Even for lunch. Yes, that's how it was. I'm telling you. That's just how it was, said Benia, smiling sadly.

What about morello cherries in chocolate, what do you say to that? We'll have a feast, said Henryk, trying to overcome the pain.

I paid up and I'm waiting. The young lady who did our nails is buying them for me in town and she'll bring them.

The volunteer? asked Leokadia. Her face muscles were twitching.

That's right, confirmed Henryk, cheering up.

What a splendid idea! I underestimated you, said Helena happily.

Morello cherries in chocolate are heavy on the stomach. They're not for us anymore, my dears, not for us, said Leokadia, painfully pulling on her gloves. Faded, blood-red suede, with a button on the wrist. I bought cherries in chocolate for the downstairs neighbor. I also left some money for the pigeons. She's going to scatter semolina for them each morning. Just as if I were there.

And does she want to be burned or buried? whined Benia. She stood up. Shifted from foot to foot.

Morello cherries in chocolate, you folks remember? Morello cherries in chocolate, huh? Wrapped in gold foil. Morello cherries in chocolate, you folks remember? said Henryk quickly, over and over, joyfully clapping his hands.

His joy spread to everyone. Apart from Leokadia, for whom the mere memory of cherries in chocolate weighed on her stomach.

You never know with the rain. You never know a thing, muttered Benia, putting her fingers to her peeling cold sores.

Helena was listening to something. She sat still in her chair. She could hear it clearly, water bubbling in her body. It was coming up abruptly, higher and higher. It was growing rhythmically, humming, as if a great tide were rising inside her body. Every splash raced against its echo, overlapping with the next sound. It was gathering fast. Undermining her. It hurt. It was pinching her skin with great force. Undermining her liver, her heart, rinsing out her entrails, scouring the inside of her mouth. She was drowning. Helena cringed. One of the waves engulfed her. The whirl reached her body and flung it into the vortex.

A smell of moistened dust arose on the terrace. The sunlight appeared diffuse. Powdery. Luminous. Like brocade. Or crushed glass. It glowed phosphorescent above the weary heads of the residents.

Benia had been singing all morning, endlessly humming a single line: Sunny meadows, lots of corn, let us jump across the tarn.

The cleaner was washing down the terrace. She had come with her child. The boy was badly overweight, which made him shy. He spent the whole time gazing at Leokadia.

Children always look at me. I'm told it's a sign of a good aura. Angelic, she said benignly. She smiled slowly at the child. But suddenly remembered her brown gums. She shielded her mouth with a hand and pretended to be yawning.

If you had a different wig he wouldn't be staring like that, advised Benia. Helena has a nice one, but as we know, she's a rich Jew. Sunny meadows, lots of corn, let us jump across the tarn.

Helena is my own sister. And she never wears a wig. That's her own hair. And don't think I can't afford a better one. I've grown accustomed to it. In the past, when there was nothing but vinegar in the stores, I had a folding toothbrush. Everyone envied me. But now what. Nothing but illnesses. It's so hot, I didn't sleep all night. I thought the end had come. I took my pulse, almost a hundred per minute, really, whimpered Leokadia quietly.

I have a pulse like a rabbit too, what can you do, said Miron, turning a cookie in his fingers. And the heartbeat, barely twenty. Slow. Very slow. As if dragging behind more and more. Out of tiredness.

Out of disgust at all this. Out of disgust, said Henryk. With the back of his hand he wiped his tear glands, as swollen as a deer's during the rut.

The heart. What's it for, and for whom? And the buzzing in my head, said Miron, dunking the cookie in a bowl of milk.

Big deal, everyone has buzzing, said Bożydar, poking dirt from under his fingernail with a knife. When there's no television, a blank screen appears in your head. But they won't consider the petition. It's a month since I submitted it.

But it depends what's buzzing. What's buzzing? In my case it's like rail tracks after a fast long-distance train. It buzzes and rings, said Miron, continuing the theme. He lisped. He sucked the cookie, heavy with milk. He took no notice of the crumbs. They fell on his shirt, stained by yesterday's soup.

And the sea keeps lapping in my skull. Not just a puddle. But a foreign ocean. Cape Horn, for instance, announced Henryk. He was sweating on his broad neck, ringed by a collar of blubber. His gaunt face stuck out of the fat like a sickly self-sown plant.

Consul, you always have to be the best. You even brag about your illnesses.

I won't let my life become vulgar. Not even here, especially here, said Henryk, wiping the inside of his sweaty hand against his suit pocket.

What is your name? Sunny meadows, lots of corn, let us jump across the tarn. I can't remember, said Benia, questioning a resident who was bustling around on the terrace with a kitchen cloth in his hand. Despite stamping his feet, he stayed in the same spot. He looked as if he were lost. His face was puffy. Covered in a network of dark red veins.

Aluś. Alinek. Aleczek, go home! For a bowl of soup, a bowl of soup, he grunted.

Aha, now I'll make something up, said Benia happily. Aleksander—a little boy. Arkadia—a little girl. It'll be easier to remember. Sunny meadows, lots of corn. And do you always go around with that cloth? Let us jump across the tarn. The nurse said your wife killed herself by putting her head in the oven. Is that right? she asked in a sing-song tone.

He confirmed it with a nod. He smiled, and showed the cloth.

Ah, I understand. She put the cloth underneath her head. But to think she had no fear of God. And afterward, was she as stiff as that cloth? Let us jump across. Yes, the nurse told me the whole story. Sunny meadows, lots of corn.

Because I told the nurse lady about it, remarked Aleksander politely.

Why not go off to your room now. You must sleep. Get plenty of sleep. You'll live a long time, ordered Benia.

All right. All right, if you please, he agreed. He set off toward the entrance gate. He latched onto the railings. He'd spend fifteen minutes at a time standing there, greeting the rare cars by bending his legs at the knees.

Sunny meadows, lots of corn, let us jump across the tarn.

A brief silence fell.

Henryk was the first to speak: Apropos female emotionality. I read about a woman who was so afraid of death that she tried to commit suicide.

Miron laughed hoarsely: Wham-bam, we're gonna buy the farm. Women always come up with things to worry about. He looked as if he were suffering badly from nausea.

It was like that with my first wife. Now I know, said Henryk, exposing his face to the sun. Not much of it was reaching him. The parasol provided a lot of shade. Especially in the afternoon hours.

You men have trouble understanding that it's possible to have an internal life, said Helena.

Do you folks know that my son is just about done with his renovation? said Benia brightly. He's promised me an orthopedic mattress. From abroad. Let us jump across the tarn.

I feel weirdly cold inside. I guess it'll be a little cooler tomorrow, observed Leokadia, wrapping herself in a shawl.

Well, it's so hot my guts are pretty much boiling, said Miron, scratching the back of his head. He stood up. He crushed a cube of dry bread. With his shoe, like an insect. He struggled to take a couple of steps. But then more and more confidently shuffled toward the building.

I admire our Miron for his bladder control, said Leokadia, taking a handkerchief from her sleeve. My tears are flowing as if the wind were gusting, she explained, wiping her eyes.

And mine too. Mine too, said Benia, nodding. She scratched her head. The hairs ran between her fingers like dried-out lumps of sand.

With each day life became less perceptible for the residents. Perhaps that was why they liked it when the staff had a lot to do with them. They wanted to be washed, brushed, touched, questioned, stripped of their pullovers, and wrapped in a rug at night. They longed to be asked about their health, about their darling, clever children, about their late lamented husbands and wives. They also knew how to listen. When the caregivers confided their troubles in them, the residents were very happy. They wanted to hear news from the other side of the wall. It made them feel as if they were still on that side of it.

It was different for Helena. She didn't like having someone take care of her, help her, or touch her. She was proud of being able to do everything for herself. Always smartly dressed. In a taffeta dress the color of red wine that concealed her anti-varicose pantyhose. Flared, so the diapers didn't show. She backcombed her hair and pinned it up—only on one side, because she hadn't the strength anymore. She'd had to give up her wedge-heeled patent leather shoes. She hadn't bent over for several years, and her feet had grown wide and misshapen, like flippers.

She squeezed the rubber bulb attached to her bottle of perfume. She sprayed scent on her neck. Her powder was forming clumps and getting stuck in the wrinkles on her neck. She was ready for an evening chat. But no one had come to see her yet. Though she had so many photos to show. From banquets, balls, and exclusive parties at mountain hostels in the days when she used to swish along on skis, overtaking everyone on the slopes, even the men.

Helena felt like knocking on someone else's door instead. If only the French language teacher. But she couldn't do it. That strange smell was coming from all the rooms she passed on her way to the dining room, that odor she had sensed the moment her stepdaughter brought her here. She could even smell it in Leokadia's room. She'd bought her perfume, and rose-scented talc, but nothing helped. And whenever Leolka came into her room to sit a while before they went to sleep, she left that smell on her bed, her dresses, and curtains. Then she couldn't sleep. One had too many thoughts about what had happened in the past. So once again she had to refuse her sister. Let her stay in her own room.

She looked in the mirror. The powder highlighted the deep lines on her face. Her gray-green eyelids had trouble opening and closing. Puffy, covered in a network of little red veins that make-up couldn't conceal.

She spent hours gazing in the mirror. Looking at the comb as it smoothed her hair. She felt as if the daytime and the waking hours had dwindled. The birds, just like her, didn't sleep. They called out to each other at night. Hopped onto the windowsills. Strolled up and down. Pattered. Peeked inside the rooms. Cocked their heads. Stared intently, and then rapidly flew off into the darkness. She was tired, very tired. She was overflowing with tiredness. He was approaching her again. Dr. Josef. Swarthy. Heaven's equal. Absent. Insubordinate. Deaf. He'd whistle as he walked across the camp. He'd stop. Rustle his starched gown. He didn't touch anything. Pointed with a gloved hand. Told her to sit on the dissection table. Showed that she was to stretch out, stay put on the metal top, in the dried blood excreted by others. He'd come close to her, no longer needing to study the nocturnal unrest of migratory birds shut in cages, or cut up the brains of rabbits stunned by a cobbler's mallet, now he had her. Now he was standing over her. In a few weeks her body would be a sack swollen with unhealthy lymph, and, shaded by a cape of matted hair, her head would wobble on her frail neck. She was here in order for him to hate himself. He could only make himself comfortable inside her, with a scalpel, a needle, bacteria. With a probe. Wriggle inside her. Reach in. Cut into. Cut open. Plunder. Cut out. Provoke swellings. Abscesses. It was good if it bled. Let the murky liquid flow out of her, dirty, stinking of gasoline.

The night refused to end, Helena couldn't get to sleep, she lay stretched out, uncomfortably stiff. She put on the radio quietly. She tried listening to the music. Once an hour they interrupted the program to broadcast the news. Once an hour she heard the same news. She wanted the buses to wake her, as in the past. They used to stop beneath her window, the doors would crash open and shut, the engine would roar.

At dawn she sat up in bed. She thought someone was walking past the door. She wasn't mistaken. She could clearly hear footsteps, then a man's voice in high spirits.

They're not to shave her. I'll need the hair for my research.

She shuddered, and someone screamed. A fitful shriek, like the trill of a nightjar, racing along the corridors, rising. Fading.

Next day, as she let her gaze stray across the tiny, wrinkled bodies of the residents, it was impossible to tell which of them could have emitted that roar.

July was in full flow, from early in the morning the sky poured heat, heavy and wooly. Even the sickest residents were silent, nobody had the strength to complain or moan.

Leokadia was keeping an eye on her sister, who felt better and was coughing less. She had taken off her sunglasses, and to avoid mislaying them she had put them in the black sequined bag where she kept her pills, handkerchiefs, and photos, of her husband and of her apartment, taken a week before leaving home.

Some of the residents were looking forward to cherries. They wanted cherries. We'll be good, we'll eat unaided, they kept repeating. You won't have to clean the tables, bibs, faces, hands. We'll help each other, serve the food, wait on the tables, suck each pit for ages, then neatly put it in a bowl. Someone had submitted a request for cherries to which they'd added the money for a gadget to remove the pits.

But once again strawberry compote was served for lunch, sweet and cloudy. They drank it reluctantly, out of constraint, lying that it tasted bitter, with every sip it tasted more bitter.

They brought in a new resident. Who'd had an amputation. Straight from the hospital. A few months ago her daughter had found her injured, with her foot gnawed by a rat.

Helena was hoping for news from the world outside, but the woman didn't say a word. She wouldn't let anyone come near. Or touch her. She stared at the residents, following them with her gaze.

Leokadia always got up early. Each morning she'd look in on the centenarians, the oldest residents. Then she'd plod off to find two deck chairs. She wanted to sit near her sister. Luckily Helena was doing less walking now. She was spending most of the day in a chair, occasionally marking time in the air.

Leokadia wanted to smell her subtle perfume, to hear her prattling, planning, provoking the other residents. Then she did less brooding. Nothing was happening in Helena's world either, but she was always able to imagine things were different. Just like the other day, when she'd brought a postcard onto the terrace, which she'd received at Easter last year from her stepdaughter.

Do you like this card? It's nice. Go on, Leolka, say it's nice.

Very nice. So colorful. Makes you want to live. Beautiful.

The priest has promised to take us into town. Just the two of us. None of those other old coots who get car sick. Just the two of us. They can stay here and shuffle around. The terrace will do for them.

Really? He's promised?

Yes, but it's a secret. Top secret. He'll smuggle us out in his car, said Helena, watching as Leokadia smoothed the bulging surface of a button.

The postcard is truly charming.

Helena agreed. Her hands, enlarged by arthritis, laboriously, wearily, pushed the button through its hole.

It's a good thing you transferred the apartment to the foundation, and they organized this home for us. Do you know how hard it is to get in here? People write applications and present references, but it's no use.

Szymon came up to the sisters. He stopped. He began to whistle very softly.

Something's been whispering inside me, he revealed, sitting down beside Leokadia. It was a loud whisper, booming in my brain. Go on, shout something. Swear and cuss, go hang yourself. Go on, more. Spit. Sin. Go to hell. Hang yourself on your belt. Slash your throat. You're such a big hero, huh? Do it to Christ, do it, he muttered, tugging at his leather belt.

Would you be so kind as to go sit somewhere else? asked Helena, vainly struggling with the air in her lungs to produce a distinct voice.

What? said Szymon, gazing at her blankly, as if he'd never seen her before.

My sister and I have something to discuss.

Szymon let his head droop. He spoke fast, rubbing the palms of his hands together like an insect.

Swear and cuss, go hang yourself. Go on, more. Spit. Sin. Go to hell.

Get away from me, you old fart. Off to the common room with you, scram, shouted Helena, and the effort brought on a coughing fit.

Szymon fell silent. He went on sitting there, with a fierce, stubborn look on his face.

Szymon, I'll talk to you later, all right? You can tell me about your momma, about Cutie, and the plankton you used to buy for him, all right? And I'll tell you about my pigeons, proposed Leokadia.

Do it to Christ, do it, said Szymon, nodding. He got up and toddled toward the building.

That's what happens when people convert but they don't have God in their hearts, quipped Helena, tidying the hair behind her ear.

You mustn't talk like that, Helena. You mustn't. We must all stick together. This is our family now. Helena, why do you tell everyone you were Miss Auschwitz?

Out there, by the lake, it must be very pretty now. I'm not in the least afraid. Just think. Summer by the water.

In search of shade, the birds were hiding in the treetops; the grass was getting thinner, and everything seemed faded, washed out, blurring at the edges. The annual flowers were wilting in their boxes. The rubber plants trapped in clay pots were losing color, going yellow, and the new shoots of a vine had stopped growing; solidified on the fence, they looked the same as last year's old, dry ones.

The menu was usually copious at this time of year. The vegetable garden behind the building supplied cucumbers, tomatoes, lettuce, and zucchini. But this year, in late June, the local council had issued a regulation on saving water. Nothing had survived the drought. Even the usually fat, fleshy lawn in front of the terrace had bald patches here and there, and clumps of dried out, faded grass.

Most of the staff had gone on vacation. And so had the man who delivered fresh food, so until early September they would have to eat more spreads, preserves, and canned fruit than usual.

The afternoon nap seemed endless, as the residents sat on the terrace with a blank look on their faces. They stared into space, their eyes fevered, their faces flushed with heat, their bodies covered in bruises from injections and IV drips, wearing clothes that were too warm, faded, and out of fashion.

There was not much talking. They had stopped complaining about their health, their fellow residents' offenses, the laziness of the staff, and the cruelty of the nurses.

It was different for Henryk. From one day to the next, to everyone's surprise, he joined the group of residents who spent all day looking for something. They'd shake out their pockets, peek under cushions, behind the curtains, in closets, beds, or waste bins. But if asked, they couldn't remember what it was they were looking for.

Someone has stolen my ivory-handled knife for cutting up the newspapers, he lamented, his soft, tearful voice faltering, splitting the words.

They don't bring us the newspapers, what do you need a knife for? Anyway, it's sure to turn up, consoled Leokadia, trying to grab Henryk's hand.

In silence he stared at Leokadia reproachfully, as if he'd never seen her before.

Ivory. From Kenya. For the newspapers. You're not listening, you uneducated morons, he shouted, sweating. Ivory. Exotic. A knife. A souvenir from Africa, he repeated more quietly. Exotic. A knife. A souvenir.

How weird that your things are always being stolen. But none of mine are, said Miron.

Because I have property, screeched Henryk. While you have nothing but the memory of your son. A lousy bum with no honor, who abandoned his wife and children, he thundered, getting out of breath.

Miron stared to one side, his gaze not resting on anything in particular, his eyeballs, penetrating space, slid torpidly, now here, now there, like a bird drifting on the waves.

So how did yesterday's visit go, Consul? asked Miron.

What visit?

That visit. To your pal who bit the dust months ago.

What are you trying to insinuate?

Don't you remember? Yesterday, after supper, you wanted to go visit your friend, the botanist, who died before Christmas, explained Leokadia.

Slander. He's alive and in good form. He's doing great.

Consul, are you seeing things or what. You won't find him in the centenarians' room or even in the house by the lake. He's pushing up the daisies, that's what, said Miron, laughing, the corners of his mouth rising in a sad smile. Just like the one that lurked on the face of Helena's husband when she pushed him away.

One day in September, several years after the war; the summer had been hot, oppressive, and only the close of August had brought rain.

Helena was sitting at the railway station in Wrocław. She was waiting for her husband, who had gone to buy snacks for the journey and a small gift for his daughter. They were on their way home from a vacation. A couple of weeks earlier she had come out of the hospital. She was told she'd been completed. The German prosthesis matched her complexion. By now she had come to terms with losing her arm. She was beautiful. Even without an arm. The year before, she'd blown out the candles on her name-day cake. She could laugh out loud. She'd bought three lengths of material for dresses. And she'd stopped hiding heels of bread in the dirty linen basket or the electricity meter box.

The vacation hadn't been a success, she couldn't enjoy the countryside; the stubble fields were mournful, the milk smelled of animal hair, the pears of putrefaction. A walk in the orchard was tiring, her shoes kept sinking into fruit that had split hitting the ground. The smell of the pigsty was everywhere. There were children shouting, chasing each other nonstop. Nosy stares. As soon as she put a foot on the threshold dogs began to bark.

She pretended to be happy. For his sake; he'd almost had a heart attack when he'd learned she was at risk of amputation. He was afraid to leave the house alone. He stayed close to her. They'd packed their bags and traveled to the mountains.

Joyfully he'd kissed her on the hair for no longer being afraid to board a train, not noticing the smell of chlorine in the coach, and letting herself be stroked on the knee. He'd thought that after a few days in the countryside they'd make love, but he was wrong.

And now she was sitting at the station, waiting for him to come back; the bench was hard, uncomfortable. Her coat was soaked through. She got up. Took it off. Laid it on the suitcases. She didn't feel cold. For a while she listened to the rain. Water hitting the roof.

He was sitting opposite. Dressed in gray. Prematurely aged. Tired. Cheeks furrowed by deep wrinkles. As if someone had ripped his face with their fingernails. The pince-nez had been replaced by thick horn-rimmed spectacles. Easier to hide behind.

First he noticed her. She could sense him staring at her. He smiled when she turned toward him. His gaze was fingering her body. Breasts, arms. It didn't recognize the prosthesis. It slid down, unpeeling the line of her thin legs beneath the fabric of her dress.

He hadn't recognized her. He was looking at her as a woman.

She kept her eyes on him. The plastic hand tightened on her thigh. And the healthy one pulled up the cotton, baring her thigh to reveal the number.

He saw it. He didn't react. He leaned back and took a newspaper from his jacket pocket. He smoothed it out. Briefly he tried to read. But he soon folded it, any old how, crookedly, and pushed it behind his suitcase strap. He straightened up. He didn't look at her. She could sense that he was shocked. He'd blocked her way so many times: Ah, so this is Hauptsturmführer Mengele's little beauty, he'd say with a laugh.

She stood and went up to him.

It's me. Hauptsturmführer Mengele's little beauty.

He didn't react.

Hauptsturmführer Mengele's little beauty. Dr. Hans. You recognize me.

She was standing in front of him, about a yard from his sharp knees, she could see the tension in his jaw. And the hesitation: whether to break free or stay put.

Dr. Hans had preferred to supervise the work of the ovens, while Dr. Josef chose to run among the new arrivals, looking for dwarves, twins, the hunchbacked and the deformed. They made a fine pair. Dr. Hans took Dr. Josef's shift whenever his wife came to see him. He didn't like to watch the blood trickling into the test tube. Nor did he like the Little Nightingale's singing or the dwarves' performances. He'd walk about the hospital, looking out of thc window and talking to Dr. Martina. Now, years on, at the station in Wrocław, he still had the air of a high school teacher. Bangs combed to one side falling over his eye. A vacant look. Fine hands, that he wasn't hiding behind black gloves anymore, nails carefully trimmed.

She was probing him with her gaze, as a predator probes its victim, before the attack.

Dr. Hans.

My name is Dr. Peltz, he said, his voice controlled. He looked up. He wasn't afraid to look her in the face.

She started screaming. She tore off his spectacles, that weakened him. As if he had surrendered, wanted her to kick, scratch, and spit at him.

My name is Dr. Peltz, he introduced himself just as calmly when two militiamen and her husband came running. He didn't even stand up. He didn't ask for his spectacles. He tidied his bangs and took out his documents.

I am a German citizen. I asked for matches. Unfortunately I forgot where I am. I asked in German. I don't know Polish. German—perhaps that caused offense and an outburst of aggression. I can understand that. Of course I won't press charges. We Germans will have to live with it for a long time to come.

Her husband and a militiaman tried to keep her at a distance, she tore free, spat, lost a shoe. And the prosthesis.

Ernst Peltz, the militiaman read from the document certifying the man's identity. What is your occupation?

I am a doctor. I practice my profession in Lower Saxony. I do not have a private surgery. I run a public inoculation service for the Department of Health.

But that could be him. He's a doctor, Helena's husband tried to break through her screams.

That's garbage. Nonsense, he said, smiling. Not every doctor was a fascist. Here's a license to practice my occupation issued by the British occupying forces, he said, taking papers from a brief-case and showing them. And also a certificate of morality. I have with me a letter from Professor Martin Staemmler, director of the Institute of Pathology in Wrocław. Before the war I began work on my doctoral degree within his faculty.

We're sorry that . . . You can understand, Doctor, explained the militiaman.

I won't lodge a complaint, but I don't want to be exposed to another attack.

We'll take care of the lady. She's a sick person. You must understand that, said the militiaman in German, returning the papers.

As they were leading her away, ignoring her shouts, he stood up. He bent down and picked up his spectacles.

She refused to leave the militia post at the station. They summoned an ambulance, they gave her an injection.

They let her make a statement. A young man in uniform questioned her without much care.

We'll report this higher up. Many people are sure to try to contact you. Although. You know what, madam, you're not the first. Plenty of citizens think they've seen SS-men somewhere. There have even been cases of innocent people being beaten up. Tourists persecuted. I don't like Germans either, but you know how it is.

It was him.

There are relevant authorities for this. We have the man's details here. He didn't run away. He let us check his identity.

Once they were home she wrote to the Lower Saxony Chamber of Physicians. A friend who knew German helped her. Nobody wrote back.

But a few years later she received an anonymous letter from Germany, type-written, in Polish. On top-quality writing paper. She scanned it quickly. She guessed the sender must work at the Lower Saxony Chamber of Physicians. He had read her letter, but for reasons not stated he was only replying now.

In several carefully composed sentences he advised that, following a trip to Wrocław in April 1962 for the purpose of collecting copies of documents relating to his pre-war academic work at the university there, for health reasons, without previous arrangement with the Chamber of Physicians, Dr. Ernst Peltz had left, along with his assistant. So far it had not been possible to establish his whereabouts. Earlier on, when he arrived from an unknown place and began his practice, rumors had appeared. At a fête held by the Lerchenhausen equestrian association a row had blown up. One of the guests had accused him of not being a doctor. Yet he did have the relevant documents and certificates. He performed his work extremely carefully. The patients liked him and people wondered why he didn't try to open a private practice. It seemed he wasn't interested in money. He spent all his spare time in the paddock with his horses. He taught his nephews to ride when they came to stay with him for their annual summer holiday. The children weren't liked. They didn't return greetings and they were very similar to Uncle Arvid, as they called Dr. Peltz.

More and more often the doctor was summoned twice a day. The residents complained endlessly about the high temperatures. About breathlessness. Cold feet. Shivering. Night sweats. Painful prickly heat. Chafing. They moaned. Whined. Sniveled. Panted. Melted. Dwindled. Their hair and wigs stank. Speckled with dirt. Moldering. Crumpled. They had stopped reminiscing. They weren't expecting their relatives to visit. Many of them had colds, though the staff watched out for drafts.

Helena complained of acute pain in her chest, but wouldn't let the doctor touch her. Her legs bent, her head hanging like a broken puppet's, she clung to the door frame and watched the doctor running down the corridor. He'd nibble the cakes on the stand set out in the entrance hall and be gone, he'd jump into his car, and turn it around with a squeal, almost joyfully.

Helena had noticed that her sister was still able to enjoy the summer. Leokadia spoke of the marvelous Augusts of the past. The blackbirds would whistle and flit from branch to branch. You could buy greengages, apricots, and plums the color of eggplants. You'd eat them on the spot, among the stalls. The juice would trickle down your fingers.

She listened to these stories in silence, without interest. She remembered the French journalists she had let into her home. She'd invited the television crew from France into her apartment, hadn't she? But they weren't interested in Dr. Hans. They only asked about Dr. Mengele. There were plenty of beasts in uniforms, but for people to be able to believe in it, that monster had to have a single face.

She confirmed that she'd spent time in the hospital barrack under the direct supervision of Dr. Josef.

Are you sure it was him? they asked, looking at the interpreter. A young girl in sunglasses.

Yes, I'm sure, replied Helena.

Maybe you just thought that? Many prisoners want to give their suffering a higher meaning, and start putting it around that Mengele himself experimented on them.

It was him.

We won't hide the fact that in some of the witness statements, those of the dwarves, for instance, some rather surprising themes appear, suggesting that if they hadn't been Dr. Mengele's guinea pigs they'd certainly have ended up at the crematorium. Being subjected to medical tortures saved their lives and they survived.

I cannot describe myself as a survivor, she replied.

That didn't interest them. She started speaking in capital letters. They weren't concerned about Dr. Hans, who had apparently been sitting around at the station in Wrocław with total impunity. They had already wasted lots of tape on similar stories. They were after Dr. Josef.

They didn't forget about her, and a few years later she received a parcel from them. A book with a dedication. An international bestseller. Her story was in there, she hadn't rattled on at them, it was enough for one paragraph.

And what about Dr. Martina, the anthropologist, did you come across her at the camp?

Many times. She gave my sister, Leokadia, a flower guide.

Your sister refuses to talk to us. Please persuade her.

She refuses to talk to me about it either.

Did you know that before the war Dr. Martina showed Mengele around Lwów? He had recently graduated in philosophy and anthropology, and she was a promising academic.

No, I didn't know that. I know he looked out for her at the

camp. She was carrying stones. She was promoted. She was his right hand. She had an office opposite the ramp. She saw everything through the window.

How do you know that?

I was in that office. With the Little Nightingale and a child whose crimped ear the doctor had spotted. The Little Nightingale was a child prodigy. A pupil of Lyuba Levitskaya. She gave singing lessons to talented children in the ghetto. She was only twenty something herself. She used to play with them. She taught the Little Nightingale a song, *Tsvey Taybelech*, *Two Little Turtledoves*, in Yiddish. Dr. Josef loved that song too. He'd say: Sing the lullaby. The Little Nightingale instantly knew which one he meant. Though it wasn't a lullaby at all. But a jaunty, jolly tune. Just the thing for a walk to the oven.

The interpreter suddenly broke off, and asked Helena: I'm sorry, but why are you watching me like that? I can't concentrate. I'm losing the thread.

Can you take off your glasses? There's no sun in this room, asked Helena.

They're only slightly tinted. I'm prone to conjunctivitis, she said, smiling, and looking at the French people. She took off her spectacles, put them down beside the tape recorder and tidied her hair.

You have lovely eyes, said Helena.

Thank you. They really are a touch unusual.

One seems more like green, and the other.

Yes, the right one is blue. It looks a bit funny, but admittedly, some men say it's interesting too, she said, glancing at the French, who were conferring on their next questions.

You'd have been interesting to Dr. Mengele too. He had a whole collection of eyeballs. Every few weeks he sent a box full of them to Germany.

But I'm not a Jew, said the interpreter, putting on her glasses.

No matter. Your eyes are unusual anyway. Dr. Josef wouldn't have overlooked them.

The manager couldn't bear the heatwaves: Yesterday someone robbed somebody again. To think that all you ladies and gentlemen come from wealthy families. It'll be best if you hand everything over for safekeeping. At this point I'd like to remind you what happened to Róża, whose fingers were so rapidly twisted by arthritis that her rings wouldn't come off. They dug into her. Broke the skin. She suffered greatly. She passed away in her family jewelry, but also in agony. Is that really necessary? Don't imagine that when at last you die your dear, inconsolable family will finally show up here. No way. More and more often nobody shows up for the corpse. We have to buy a new plot in the municipal cemetery. None of you wants to lie in a common pit, do you. Or maybe you want your fingers cut off, chop chop, after your demise?

A legitimate point. Most thoughtful, agreed Henryk. Where are the days when the bodies of the dead were caressed with linen bands and their innards filled sarcophagi.

Henryk, I'm looking forward to another poem on the matter, said the manager, grimacing with laughter.

Is it true they've closed our branch by the lake? asked Leon.

That's baloney—it's bursting at the seams. They don't know what to do with the residents. And one more thing, I've received a petition about watching movies at night. Nice idea, but it's extremely stuffy in the common room, and I guess none of you folks wants to march off to purgatory in your worn-out slippers in front of the TV. So for now the common room will be closed in the daytime too. The way it is, we're obliged to protect you, not pander to all your whims, said the manager, checking the state of his tire with two kicks. He then got in the car and drove off.

Hell and damnation. One–nil, said Bożydar angrily. I won't give up. I'll write a new petition for them to let us use the shower rooms more often. And one shampoo for twenty is not enough.

It's already too late to be afraid, said Leokadia.

Helena watched her sister in silence. She thought about her own hair. Thick. Abundant. With wavy coils of rust-and-amber ringlets on her shoulders. Dr. Josef had allowed it to get longer and longer. He'd take it in his glove-coated hand. He'd dig around in her curls. Run his fingers through them. Pull hard. He was surprised it didn't fall out. He'd tug and tug. It remained strong and healthy. But when he told her to lie on the stretcher for photographs, her hair was to be smoothly pressed to her skin, hidden behind her back. Otherwise the flesh that had been experimented on would not be fully visible. The photograph wouldn't work. The ulcerated, scalpel-slashed arm absolutely had to be in the foreground.

She used to close her eyes. She didn't want to look at the human skins. They hung on a line outside the laboratory. Like laundry.

Here was a reward for the little beauties. On first inspection they were just children. Worthless human material that couldn't work productively. If they fitted in a bucket of water, that was where they ended up. The bigger ones could lie on the dissecting table and they had to be injected with phenol. Or hydrogen. But then there was a twenty-minute wait for loss of consciousness and death. Though the time could be spent on conversation. It was nice to chat, ask about Momma and the name of their little brother.

Dr. Josef was overworked. They brought him so many children. Chilled to the bone. Famished. Sick. They weren't even fit for broth. Not so their fathers. They were ideal for *Menschenbouillon*. The flesh was cut off the thighs and arms. Boiled, cooled and used to feed the bacteria in the laboratories. What remained, the fresh material from the liver, pancreas, and spleen, was collected, secured, and retained.

Helena could have been a human object. But Dr. Josef liked to touch her on the belly with his crop. She was proud of her skin. No blemishes, ulcers, stretch marks, or purulence. I wouldn't have been big enough to make jodhpurs, but I'd have done for a pair of gloves, a wallet, a small, exquisite, ladies' coin purse, or to cover a book, a volume of poetry, or part of a lampshade. The rest could be added on. Made out of other Miss Auschwitzes. They lay beside her. Naked. With pendants ending in metal plates with the same number as the non-human guinea pigs assigned to them.

Here was a reward for the little lovelies. A major victory for Miss Auschwitz. She could share blood, pus, and bacteria with her guinea pig. Both were in pain. As if joined by a placenta. They swelled up. Lost their hair. Something would be rotting away in there. Something would be falling off. Slowly. In small pieces. And the next photograph. A chest cut open. A burned groin. A hot substance from the anus and the vagina.

Her husband's touch reminded Helena of Dr. Josef's assistant fingering her. They did it in just the same way. With curiosity. Tenderly. With a trembling, avid hand. He liked her hair smoothed down. Gathered back. He wanted to comb it. She'd throw it over her shoulder so it hung over the back of her chair, almost to the ground. He was very careful. He'd take hold of one strand at a time. He'd gently hook the comb into it and slowly slide it downward. She was sure he could feel her trembling. Being afraid.

August was very hot.

Dry as a bone. Not a drop of rain. At night it was impossible to breathe. The temperature only dipped a few degrees. The television forecast the worst heat wave for years.

Because of the regulation on saving water, the residents were bathed in groups of five. Undressed, their bodies were soaped by a hand armed with a sponge mitt, then hosed down. Those in wheelchairs were seated on ordinary chairs, old, chipped, creaking, and warped by damp.

The residents were more frequently coughing, spitting, soiling themselves, and excreting in a corner, a nook in the corridor, or in the treatment room when the nurse had gone out for a moment. Many of them were complaining of matted hair, chafing in the groin, and ears blocked with wax. But thorough hygiene would only be addressed once the heat had abated and some of the staff were back from their vacation.

Occasionally someone passed a stool behind the manager's car. The hot weather was not conducive to rational decisions.

A story started doing the rounds of the residents—Irena had broken the rules about saving water, and soaked her underwear in a bowl. She'd tripped, fallen face first into the water. And drowned.

A funny death, but a death, said Henryk, nodding, as he fumbled in the folds of his rug in search of his ivory-handled knife.

I'm weaker and weaker. I'm just a bother to you all. I want to die now. It's time to say goodbye. Time I was off to purgatory, Benia complained to the nurse.

Benia, what are you saying? Having a bad time here? It's even worse in purgatory. No one knows what penance they'll get.

Benia, you were born, you raised your kids, it's high time you strutted off to paradise, advised Miron. His hands were flying around, and so was the spittle, snot-green, stuck to his shirt.

It's so hot. It's so hot, said Helena, wiping her perspiring brow. It's harder to breathe by the hour, harder to walk, and eating is unthinkable. Even my voice feels alien to me, she muttered to herself.

The caregiver suggested water. She had a similar voice to the woman who'd called her long after the war. A soft female voice trained to show sympathy.

Would you like to have your photographs? she'd asked.

What photographs?

From the camp. They might come in useful for compensation. They're sure to pay out some more. We've accumulated more than fifty thousand photos. The photographer survived. We have a sizeable collection.

I don't want. Any photographs.

But it's proof. The best proof. Not like oral accounts. Proof. You never know when it might be useful.

Who took them? Have they caught someone?

The photographs that one of the prisoners took of you.

I don't want anything.

As I've said, it'll facilitate any potential compensation.

I've already been given a prosthesis. And money. I bought myself a television set and a watch.

You never know, it might come in handy one day. Hello? Can you hear me? Are you there?

I'm hanging up, said Helena, and did it in mid-sentence.

The lamp cast a bright halo around the caregiver's head. Tiny moths were crashing into the shade, rising up, fluttering, spinning in a streak of light, and diving to where it was brightest. The night was grayish, as if misted, like fleshy velvet creased against the vault of the sky.

Deck chairs and residents. Some sat wrapped in blankets, with pillows under their heads, and stools supporting their feet. They were asleep. Or lying down at rest. Gazing indifferently at those gathered on the terrace. One's own life seemed like somebody else's.

Helena fetched a book, found seats for herself and Leokadia beside the caregiver, and listened to her steady, sleepy voice. Today, once again the residents were listening to the story of a man who fed stray cats. Stooping, he'd unwrap greaseproof paper on the roof tiles, and fetch out long strips of beef, sprinkled with sugar to enhance the flavor. Then he'd step aside to avoid scaring the animals, take a seat on a vent at one corner of the roof, on the apex—and watch as the cats came in from all directions.

The caregiver's voice was soft and tired: Thanks to the sweet shin of beef, though feral and not domesticated, the cats soon grew accustomed to the man's presence, and after a few days they started showing joy at the sight of him. They came running out in long bounds to greet him, holding their tails high, purring, and rubbing against his calves.

The caregiver broke off, because she thought Henryk was just about to stop trying to hold in his stool. But under the pressure of her gaze he calmed down.

She went on reading: But what they liked best about the man was the smell of his polyester coat, a mixed odor of sour potato malt and old fruit cores. The material was fragile and it rustled gently, the cuffs were decorated with cold buttons that made you sneeze if you put your nose to them, and reminded the cats of the mating season.

Mister Pilot, time to quit, your plane's got a hole in it, shouted Miron, leaning back and tilting his head until a fit of coughing doubled him up.

The caregiver stopped reading: What will happen next, do you folks know, or not? she asked without curiosity, loosening her hair and tying it in a ponytail again.

The cats will come in.

From all directions.

Mister Pilot, time to quit, your plane's got a hole in it.

They're hungry, and the man will feed them.

He'll bring them food, and they'll be grateful to him and contented, they replied.

Perhaps I needn't go on reading, since you know it all by heart?

They protested. As a group, loudly, showing surprising energy and willpower. Suddenly everything they thought they had lost forever was on display.

She went on reading: The cats came in from all directions, flexing and stretching their bodies as they leaped from one building to the next, from one roof to the next. The man soon learned to tell them apart. The fattest ones came right up to him.

Helena didn't have to close her eyes to imagine cobalt-blue cats with orange eyes, like ripe, meaty oranges. She could see them rubbing against the man's legs, and their eyes narrowing to show their pleasure and devotion. She began to feel sorry she hadn't had a cat. Or any pet animal ever. She wanted to remember the good things. But her mind was fixed on other memories. What a beautiful child I was, she mused, smoothing down her cream-colored calico skirt. Healthy, white skin. Yet not a single one of my veins was visible.

And my nose had no hump. It was upturned, even when I wasn't smiling, just as if my little face were laughing. My eyes were never sad either. Everyone had sad eyes—but not I. That's why I instantly became little Miss Auschwitz. At once they gave me the best bunk and clogs, clothes that weren't stained with dried blood or soiled with excrement. And they let me keep my hair. Long and fine. Like a little coat. To my knees. It was a lovely little coat. A lovely little coat with a dirty lining.

A little coat of hair, said Helena aloud.

But none of the residents was looking in her direction.

Leokadia was asleep. Her slow breathing seemed to keep stopping for longer and longer. For so long that it was hard to tell if her diaphragm would pick up its task again.

A little coat of hair, repeated Helena, looking at the residents. Withered, like parchment, bent double, thick-waisted, with swollen bellies and skin hanging like soiled jabots.

A little coat of hair. A little coat of hair.

The caregiver paused. She looked in her direction. She sighed. And returned to reading.

A little coat of hair, Helena kept repeating faster, and faster, with no one interrupting her.

She jumped to her feet. First she felt pain from such a sudden action. Then it was as if she had no body. She moved forward smoothly, shouting non-stop about her little coat of hair. She grabbed hold of the caregiver. And spat at her.

That's the payment I get for all the shit I've removed from her rear end, you see that? screamed the caregiver, throwing the book aside.

She jumped up to restrain Helena. She tried to get a firm grip on her. Hold onto her with both hands. Pull her toward herself with all her might. Embrace her. Stroke her head. Calm her down. But she failed to catch her. Helena tripped over a deck chair. And fell. The arm of the chair struck her in the belly. She slipped onto the paved walk.

Her breathing returned slowly. She inhaled sharply, in shallow gulps, sand coated her tongue. Then she saw them all. They were all looking in her direction. They knew she wasn't crying because of the fall.

The sun was so tiresome that some of the residents refused to believe the days were getting shorter.

The air was still. Sultry. The scent of the flowers intensified. Their petals were dropping abruptly, rapidly, as if torn off by the wind, and yet it was quiet. The geranium and pelargonium leaves had gone autumnally yellow.

The garden had become ugly. Neglected. The flower pots and boxes were ineffectual. A cocoon of flies quavered above the broken, leaking hose. The water in the pond resembled a puddle. Its ragged edges surrounded manes of yellow foam. The parched air vibrated above the scorched grass, quivering in the heat. On the walls blowflies basked by the thousand.

Bożydar would not give in. He kept writing petitions. Twice a day he went up to the gate. He collected the advertisements stuffed between the railings. He took them back to his room. Cut them into strips. Distributed them to the bathrooms. As toilet paper.

Apparently they've closed the house by the lake.

What are you saying, Leokadia? wondered Henryk, watching in disgust as Miron leaned over his armrest, let drop some brown spittle, followed its fall, and then contemplated the pattern it had made on the chipped floor tiles.

Apparently they've closed it, said Leokadia, nodding.

The residents started having gastric problems, the next day they were dehydrated, and then they were done for, said Miron.

What are you saying? All of them? inquired Henryk.

Every single one. They've bought the farm. Some bacteria or

something. Summer. It's no wonder. Poisoning's easy, kicking the bucket's a piece of cake, explained Miron, stretching comfortably in his chair.

And I have such weak bowels. It makes you afraid to eat, she said in horror.

You've gotta eat. While your jaw's still working, advised Miron. He shifted on his seat. His face was restless. His eyes sticky. He straightened his legs. His feet could breathe thanks to the holes he'd made in his sneakers.

Do you want to be burned? asked Benia.

It sounds as if they poisoned them over there by the lake, huh? Am I right? said Miron, glancing at Leokadia.

Yes, yes, they did. We must be very well-behaved, screeched Benia, and added, looking at Miron: You didn't answer me, do you want to be burned or. . . ?

Eight times a day I reply to you that I want to be burned and scattered over Warsaw. My dad, mom, and brothers are there. And my son. And I'll never forgive myself for not taking him on flights over the city. He loved airplanes. But I wouldn't spare him the money. I don't know what I— He broke off, tired of his own ranting.

Ah, yes, now I remember, you have already told me all that, said Benia, starting to fold and unfold a handkerchief, while struggling to catch her breath.

Miron suddenly stood up. It's bullshit about the house by the lake. Lies. All to make us afraid, he said, turning around several times, as if looking for something. Finally he waved a hand and went off to his room.

Helena sat in her chair. Without talking. Just staring ahead. At the entrance gate. When they fired her from the library, she'd gotten herself permission to go around to elementary schools giving talks. There was plenty of competition, but the committee was thrilled by her rich, lively language, her great personal charm, and the unique aura she radiated, that's what was written in the "additional comments" supporting the permit.

Once a week she went to one of the schools. By the blackboard she'd hang up her little camp uniform stained with pus and dirt. She'd show them jars filled with paper bandages. She'd unfasten her prosthesis. Show the marks on her body. Tell her story. Give the children quarters of rotten apples. Little fists of bread corroded by blue streaks of mold.

They laughed. They refused to eat. She got upset. She forced their jaws open. Pressed it into their mouths.

She was reprimanded. You can't do that. Why terrify the children? Maybe when they're older, scolded the education officer.

There were thousands younger than them in there, she said, raising her voice.

They stopped inviting her. The children couldn't sleep afterward. They were afraid to visit the hygienist. They refused to be inoculated.

Benia received a letter from her children.

Dearest Momma, be sure to eat all your food. Mind you walk around with a crutch, and if need be, a walking frame so you don't fall over. We sold your cottage long ago. As soon as you left. We spent three weeks throwing out the trash you left, because you always thought everything might come in handy. The packaging for sugar and flour, leaflets that were left by your garden gate. Bottles. Jars. We took it all out at night because we were ashamed in front of the neighbors. We had a terrazzo headstone made for Dad, and Tadeusz did so well at winning over the gravediggers that you could fit five more guys in with Dad. Please don't bicker with your fellow residents. Be nice to the nurses, and don't bother the caregivers. Eat up all your food, because the cash from your pension goes on that. We'll come visit next year in August, because right now the tractors are running well and we're all busy with that, the whole family. We're doing up the house. When you come, you won't recognize it. Love and kisses, all our very best wishes.

Benia had it read to her often. The caregivers carried out her request.

The heat softened the world and made it sticky. Couch grass was rife everywhere, coated in dust and white stains, as if from soap suds. The temperature melted any desire for conversation or a walk. Some of the residents weren't leaving their beds.

The heat sharpened the residents' features. Their cheeks sagged, the bones in their faces were almost piercing the skin. They were becoming torpid. Turning wild. Inhumanly weary. Cuticles picked at by chewed fingernails were peeling off, catheters were visible, bruises from needles, and little cuts from mosquito bites. Their skin was dehydrated, resembling parchment, it looked as if it could be separated, one layer from another, as if it were made of flimsy tissue paper.

Airing the rooms was not helping. There was a sour smell everywhere. The odor of vomit, urine, and feces, mixed with the subtle, oily fragrance of dried grass and flowers.

Someone had overheard the nurses; apparently the manager had carried out an inspection of the residents' rooms. Three times a day. It was too warm for a body to remain in bed until the morning round.

The staff are whispering about us. As if we were bedridden, said Benia, nodding.

Aren't we? sputtered Leon.

The residents told each other that the feebler ones would be taken off to the house by the lake.

Only Leokadia had recovered her good mood. We must look

as fit as a fiddle, she twittered, shielding her brown gums with a hand. Let's stroll around with books under our arms. Poetry. The classics. We can take away some mashed carrot in a little bag and smear it on our faces. It'll make us look good. Healthy and happy, she advised.

Drafts were causing infections, muscle pain, and sinus trouble. The volunteer was going around the residents' rooms, caring for their neglected bodies. She wanted to see to Helena's chafed stump too. Rub greasy fish-oil cream on it.

Helena was sitting on the bed. She was finding it hard to speak.

I don't seem to be thinking about anything, and then, all of a sudden, quite unprompted, it leaps out of nowhere: Momma. Momma, I say out loud. As if I could see her. She's been trying to summon me. As if she were here all the time, very close by, buzzing around the house. It only takes a whisper for her to come to me. She walked up. She sat down on the edge of the bed. And that was all. My momma. Momma.

Hush. Hush now. You're always so brave. It's a temporary crisis. Sure to be because of the heat wave. Everything's going to be fine, said the volunteer. She extended a hand to stroke her.

Helena pulled away. Don't touch me. Who gave you permission.

Benia was constantly asking the caregivers to read her the letter from her children. Once she knew it by heart, every resident had to hear it several times. Now she was trudging about in nothing but a rainproof coat. Polyester worn through on the seams, the Velcro had come off, there were holes.

Benia, you'll get very sweaty, commented the others.

You never know with the rain, you never know, she muttered. Straight after that she fell onto the table. Clutching a spoon, her hand looked scalped, composed of nothing but bone and sinew.

Miron stroked her head, and whispered something, while Helena plodded off to fetch help.

Fifteen minutes later the ruffled Benia was sipping sugar water, and listening to Leokadia's stories about ladybugs, the mole, and the meadow speckled with orchids.

Miron retold the latest joke doing the rounds among the residents: What's the fastest way to get to the home by the lake? Answer: In a bed on wheels.

They had trouble nodding off, and then their sleep was shallow, marred by nightmares.

Helena had a dream about the manager. He ordered a roll call. He told them to stand to attention. I won't tolerate cheating, he declared. A face may be pretty, but under those clothes death is lurking. Yes, death. Let's not be afraid of that beautiful word. So straight after breakfast the caregivers will carry out an inspection of your esteemed bodies. Let me remind you that is their job. They are professionals and they don't look at you ladies and gentlemen with the eyes of women, or people, so to speak. They're not interested in your schlongs, wieners, or other attractions. The caregivers look with the eyes of personnel. That's why you must strip naked. As for a bath. So many cosmetics, lotions, creams—it's impossible to tell who has a few more days ahead of them and who's on the point of keeling over. Preventive action is the best approach. Early detection of death—and a needle in the vein. That's nicer than death with a carrot-stained kisser.

Lying in her room at night, Benia reconstructed every word of the letter from her children. She thought of her grandson. His small, puffy lips sagged toward his chin, and there was a fleshy bump in the middle of the lower one. She was sure that just like his father he liked to chew hard candy and pencils, gnash nuts in their shells, and suck oranges through a small hole drilled with a fingernail.

Benia's eyes probed the darkness. She couldn't sleep.

A few bedrooms away Miron was dreaming of his son.

The night abruptly threw off its dark gloom, filling with light.

Here too death was being hidden, but not always successfully. Benia had fallen out of the window. She was lying on a boxwood hedge next to the drive. Thorns had scratched her cheek, hooked into her hair, and rolled up her dress. The manager and the staff were waiting for the doctor, the police, and a vehicle from the Kiss of Eden to take away the corpse.

The residents wanted to be with Benia for as long as possible.

The caregivers brought chairs so they could sit down, have a look, and say goodbye. Any deviation from the usual routine helped to ease the boredom.

She looks like in the past. You might think she's just dozed off a while.

I knew she wouldn't drag on for long. They say that when a woman who drinks stops drinking, she dies at once.

She didn't drink. How can anyone drink here. Just sugar water.

She drank, she drank. I can always recognize a woman who drinks. And when a woman who drinks stops drinking, she dies at once. So does a man who drinks too. When a man who drinks stops drinking, he dies at once.

Whenever someone dies you always say they were a drunk. How can you speak such slander against the deceased, said Leokadia indignantly.

Let's not drop our bad habits too hastily. The main thing is not to surrender to hygiene. Let's allow our cuticles to abrade at their own pace. Let's not interfere in the world of decay with a crummy pumice stone, advised Leon.

Something's been whispering inside me. It was a loud whisper, booming in my brain. Go on, shout. Swear and cuss, go hang yourself. Go on, more. Spit. Sin. Go to hell. Hang yourself on your belt. Slash your throat. You're such a big hero, huh? Do it to Christ, do it, muttered Szymon.

They were all staring at the dead woman's shoes. For the first time Benia was not wearing her misshapen knee boots with the dirty sheepskin trim. She'd put on black loafers with a raised seam decorating the toes. Glossy, badly matched shoe polish had changed the matt material into patent leather. Black, perfectly polished, they shone, mocking the solemnity of death. The soles were uneven, worn down, but clean and tidy. Not a speck of dirt. Anyone could see that an hour earlier she'd wiped herself with a sponge. Carefully combed her hair. Sprinkled her neckline with too much perfume borrowed from Helena. Even now, several hours later, its sharp smell was getting into the residents' noses, occasionally prompting one of them to sneeze and shift on their chair with a groan.

When Minxy was dying, first of all she trembled. Then she went under the radiator. She just about squeezed in between the ribs, said Leon, unable to tear his gaze from Benia.

Yes, dogs tremble for a long time first, and then wham-bam, they give up the ghost. And they're stiff. Done for already, said Miron, and laughed out loud.

Our Minxy. Well, what is there to say? Sometimes I can see her, looking at my wife with those clever little eyes of hers. Or being overjoyed when I walk in the door. She jumps up on the armchair, or the couch. She'd race around in a fit of joy. I only have to think of her and I can't fall asleep. I get up and walk around.

Why are you so gloomy? the caregiver asked Leokadia.

She didn't answer.

Isn't it high time to get used to death? So why the gloom?

She pressed for an answer, without real interest.

Only those with teeth can smile, announced Miron. And suddenly began to cry.

The caregiver took him by the arm. She stroked him. Comforted him. Led him off to his room. He toddled along, pressing close to her side, small and shriveled, in a sweatsuit gone fuzzy with wear.

For some reason I'm cold. Maybe it's from shock, said Leokadia, wrapping her arms around herself.

Well, I must admit that those who spend their emotional capital often suffer a negative balance of energy, said Leon, tugging his beard and blinking.

Has anyone seen my knife for cutting up the newspapers? An unusual one. Has anyone seen my knife? An unusual one. Exotic, inquired Henryk.

There are bullets after us, but we don't even know it, said Bożydar.

Has anyone seen my knife for the newspapers? Has anyone? Henryk went on asking plaintively, hovering among the assembled company.

We live, and then—thud. We fall, like pears in an orchard, muttered Bożydar, once again counting the signatories to his petition against the staff turning off the water in the shower rooms.

It's hard to live, but it's even harder to kill yourself. Shoot a hare—yes. That's a piece of cake. Wham-bam, job done. Does anyone remember our Benia? Fancy her jumping out the window. Benia was a very brave woman, who'd have thought it. Most of us can only dream of shooting themselves in the head.

I'd still like to go to Białystok. Where Momma was from, said Leokadia, sweating more and more.

You should have come with me that time, said Helena, standing over her sister, stooping to straighten her rolled-up collar.

But maybe it's better you didn't come, Leolka. The train stopped, but I didn't get out. I was gripping the handle of my suitcase so hard my knuckles were white. And I lost my hair, would you believe it? That was when I lost my little coat of hair. I didn't get out, I didn't move from my seat, but my hair came out of me, as if it were badly stuck to my skin. I wanted to get out.

She broke off.

The caretaker opened the entrance gate. A car with the words Kiss of Eden on the hood drove onto the lawn, gone bald in the heat.

Do you folks remember how Benia used to fall off everything? Off the steps. Off a stool? Off the edge of the terrace? That's why I'm sure it'll be just the same now. One day she'll simply fall from the sky and be back with us, said Leon.

Helena stroked Leokadia on the cheek and said:

It's good that you're not wearing your wig anymore. After all, you've still got your hair.

I'm letting my skin breathe. It's too hot. But without my wig I feel— As if I were naked, do you know what I mean? complained Leokadia.

Come on, I'll make you braids.

Helena, get a grip.

Your hair is very short. But perhaps something can be charmed out of those mouse tails, said Helena, helping her sister to get up.

They were in a hurry. They didn't want to look—two men from the Kiss of Eden were pulling Benia's diminutive body out of the boxwood hedge.

As they walked past the driver of the hearse, Helena said:

How handsome you are.

She stopped.

Oh my God, surely you're not one of the guys who transport corpses?

I used to be ashamed of having this profession. I'd tell people I drove apples instead. But now if I want to get to know anyone, I tell them straight that I transport stiffs. I bought the car with a loan. It's a special model. An Opel Admiral, he said, looking at Helena like a product at the wholesaler's to see if it's any good or not.

Am I crumpled? she asked.

You remind me of this one lady. She put a photo of herself with her breasts exposed into her husband's coffin. But somehow it didn't have much of an effect on him.

There are all sorts of ways to show our loss of a loved one, Leokadia added to the conversation.

Even the most vulgar woman can have the purest intentions, she added, nudging her sister to walk on.

I'll tell you something, said Helena, gesturing to hush her pesky sister.

You have no idea who stands before you. Who am I? You'll never guess. Miss Auschwitz. I don't neglect myself like the other widows. And I won't be taken in by the staff's tricks. Yesterday they bought us each an artificial sunflower, stuck them in sponges, and to make us human we're supposed to take care of those pieces of plastic. Even my sister does it. She waters it. Sniffs it. Loves it as if it were her own child.

Helena. Give it a break. The man's working here.

Leokadia embraced her sister.

All right, stick a fork in it, it's done, he said, and got into his car. He rolled up the window.

Please be kind to our Benia, demanded Helena.

The first thing Helena did after Benia's death was to cover the mirror in her room.

Why did you do that? asked Szymon, who for several days had been shuffling after Helena.

It's not good to look at yourself at a time of mourning, she replied reluctantly, in a weary tone.

Szymon drew the cover aside and looked in the mirror. He had a strange expression on his face. Like when someone opens a present and doesn't get what they were hoping for.

That same night Miron crept into Benia's room.

They'd cleaned it. There was no smell of Benia. A metal bed frame. A mattress covered in plastic sheeting to stop urine from soaking in. A bedside cabinet. A chair. A closet for a few coat hangers. A waste bin lined with a bag. Walls set close together. So bright and antiseptic that it looked like a cubic light box. Cleanliness christened with chlorine. For the new occupier.

Miron closed the door behind him. He leaned slightly forward, like a bird getting ready to take off. He broke wind. Then at once went pale. He took a breath, a sign of the relief he'd just felt.

On the floor, almost underneath the bed, he found some dust balls and a lost photo. He knelt down to pick it up. He wiped it with the palm of his hand. And saw a little girl, just a few years old. Chubby-cheeked. Squinting. Trusting. Smiling at the person taking her picture against a backdrop of trees. Poplars perhaps. She was hugging a dog. Black with a white muzzle. Up to the child's hips. On the back he found an inscription: Little Benia and Edyta. Fryda Micberg's boarding house. Otwock Highway. 1938.

He hid the picture under his belt and covered it with his shirt. He struggled to his feet. Coughing and hawking. He shuffled off to his own room.

They'd taken her away, and here she was again. Benia lay in the common room, which had been kitted out to look like the interior of a funeral home.

Garlands of spruce painted black. Plastic calla lilies washed and placed in crystal vases. A sign hanging from the ceiling: Farewell forever. Fly higher than the birds. Look down on us with affection. But they'd forgotten to iron it.

As a special offer the manager had gotten the latest style of coffin. With a little window opening at face height. Behind the glass, Benia looked distant, wrinkled, and proud. Like eyelashes, her hair had been curled into ringlets.

The coffin was standing on stools. Some large bowls had been pressed in between them, filled with roughly hewn chunks of ice. In view of the heat, the farewell ceremony did not last long.

Only as they said goodbye to Benia did it occur to them that they'd forgotten to ask: Was she to be burned or buried?

Helena put the little box Benia had given her into the coffin. She spent a long time keeping watch beside the deceased. She was proud of the black garland made from a Shetland wool shawl. She'd pinned silver angel hair to it, and the caregiver had draped the whole thing on a lamp.

Leon, Szymon, and Miron were sitting next to her. Dressed in stiff suits and white shirts. That's probably how they'll be buried, thought Helena. She sighed as she lowered her head. Only then did she notice that these guards in mourning were wearing slippers, misshapen, worn smooth by bow legs, by a waddling gait.

Did you know that the manager once had a child that died? said Szymon too loud, as those who are hard of hearing often do.

It only lived two days. That's why he hates us so much. I can understand him. We've had our share of life, but his kiddy never got it. Just think, two days in this world. Two breakfasts. Two lunches and two suppers. And we're still alive.

Does anyone know why exactly we're still alive? muttered Miron.

He cast a glance at Leon.

They say you have to grow into death. Some people don't take long to do it. We must wait a bit longer, announced Leon, showing them fiery eyes.

Miron, do you want to be burned or buried? asked Helena, hoping to amuse him.

She thought he was suffering. He was getting slower by the day.

Helena laid her hand on his. She gently took hold of a finger.

He pulled his hand away. The rapid movement must have caused him pain. His lips twisted into a grimace. But seconds later, when it seemed as if they weren't going to talk, he said in a whisper:

Helena, you have the effect of vodka on me. You make me want to live and all that, he admitted. His moldering face twitched.

Has anyone seen my knife? An unusual one. Exotic, said Henryk, toddling in.

He stood there, fidgeting. Reluctantly, they made room for him.

Well, own up, out with it.

He groaned once he'd finally sat down.

With a good deal of difficulty he bent over and laid his head on Helena's thigh. Then fell asleep before she could even stroke his hair.

Staring at a cadaver is one hell of a good thing, said Leon.

You suddenly notice you're still alive. Your kidneys are filtering, your heart's thumping, and your gob's gabbing, which brings saliva to the tongue. Nothing can ruin the joy of still clinging to life. The dead play an important role. They tell us we've still got something ahead of us. My dears: you still have a little time. The clock's still ticking for you. Listen to the ticking. Don't cover your ears.

Leon had distinctly lowered his voice.

Then he suddenly stopped talking, rubbed the tip of his nose, and fixed his gaze on Benia.

Benia looks better than in the past, whispered Helena.

You might think she's just nodded off, and is seeing unparalleled beauty in her dream, like that first time. I've never seen such a beautiful dead person. As if angels were caressing her. See how young she looks, her little nose, her chin and cheeks are almost like a child's. Heaven is a place where we're all beautiful.

Without death life would be so trivial, said Leon.

I knew she wouldn't drag on for long. She liked to knock it back, said someone from behind.

They say that when a woman who drinks stops drinking, she dies at once. The people on her floor say she liked a drop. Often, albeit reluctantly. So what more is there to say? he added.

But how can anyone consume alcohol here? inquired Miron with a note of resentment. It's impossible, impossible.

Let's not drop our bad habits too hastily. The main thing is not to surrender to hygiene. Let's allow our cuticles to abrade at their own pace. Let's not interfere in the world of decay with a crummy pumice stone, repeated Leon.

He stood up. Went over to the window. And briefly struggled with it. It was warped by the heat. Hot air burst in. Shut it, shut it. The ice will melt, hissed the residents.

You shouldn't have come here. The sight could do you harm, said Leokadia to her sister, stroking her head. She'd only dropped in for a moment.

Leave me be, said Helena, turning her head slowly, to avoid waking Henryk.

After all, you never did go to funerals.

See how good Benia looks in that silk shawl. I gave it to her. She was always wanting to borrow it.

Let's get out of here. Shall we go down to the roses? suggested Miron.

He started coughing, groaned, straightened up, and shuffling his slippers, left the common room.

The rest of them didn't talk. They sat tightly. One touching the next.

A few days after the Kiss of Eden had taken Benia's body away to the funeral home appointed by her family, a welcome wind arose.

The residents poured onto the terrace. They snuggled into the canvas of the deck chairs, billowing in the breeze. They wore carelessly done-up clothing. Too warm. Threadbare. Not fresh. Like museum exhibits. Their faces looked like marble, inanimate, petrified in a single grimace. Transparent. Weathered. The gaze aimed deep inside the body, a network of tiny veins exposed, a cobweb of blood vessels, bruises, blemishes, subcutaneous bleeding. Other faces were too mobile. Overstimulated. Criss-crossed. Shredded by abruptly changing emotions. They resembled animated gargoyles on the fronts of buildings.

They were looking forward to their cherries. Getting bored, they kept thinking about cherries. Complaining of the endless summer. Taking their temperature. Awaiting their families. Suffering. Looking at the pelargoniums in the boxes and the rubber plants in the pots.

Now they talked of nothing but cherries. In staccato sentences. In scraps. Syllables. Each person's favorites: large with thin skin, small, sweet, watery. Stringy, tart, like sour cherries. Or light, white or also dark, purple, fleshy, almost mealy. Pretty, compact, a pity to eat them. Shapeless, pecked by starlings. Gone bad, too moldy to eat, like a bitter, watery bladder. With tiny stones, flimsy peel. Or else huge, hard, well-padded with pulp, enveloping all the sweetness.

Henryk was no longer there. There was no one to delight with his memory of the mangoes he'd eaten in Africa. They missed his wise-guy talk about their thick, sickly-sweet juice slowly trickling down his chin.

They groaned: Cherries, our cherries. Each person wanted to tell about the ones they'd had in childhood. The men boasted of the high trees they'd climbed. Quickly. Barefoot. Knees hugging a rebellious trunk. How they'd picked the fruits from the very top, while the branches shook, bending to the ground. The women fondly remembered twin cherries. They'd hooked them on their ears. Worn them with pride, like ruby earrings. They wouldn't let each other speak. Each one wanted to be heard. Once, long ago, they had eaten the best, the most wonderful cherries. From Grandma's basket. From Grandpa's rough hands. From Momma's lips. From Father. From a lover. A fiancé. A newly married wife. A stranger.

The wind was not a herald of rain. In the afternoon it became stuffy, dense. It burned their cheeks. Blocked their mouths. Filled the larynx with sand blown in from the drive. It gave no respite. Made it impossible to breathe. Stung the eyelids. Flushed the cheeks. Overturned the deck chairs and tipped up the boxes full of withered pelargoniums. Yanked at the wilted shoots of the vines.

Some of the residents were knocked over by these gusts. For their safety they were forbidden to leave their rooms.

More and more often, Leokadia went to take a look at the oldest residents.

They lay in a large room. The staff called it the Supercentenarians' Crypt, and the manager's name for it was the Waxworks Museum.

Smoking a cigarette on the terrace one day, the priest had rashly admitted that visiting the oldest residents made him feel like Ezekiel in the Bible, led to the Valley of Dry Bones.

There were several of them. They no longer had their own furniture. The couches from the bedrooms had been replaced with hospital beds. Set on metal frames on wheels. Easy to move out. To empty. To disinfect.

It was hard to discern them. They only stood out from the folds of the bedclothes by the darker shade of their skin. Its consistency. The shadowed eye sockets. A wisp of hair. The lumps on a skull. The growths. Their roving eyes never stopped. Now and then their hands crept onto the surface. The combs of their fingers clutched the air. Like wanderers in search of immortality, avid for life. That was what Henryk told everyone about them in his poem.

They hardly ate at all. They were fed by IV drips. Until there was nothing left to stick a needle into. They couldn't sit up without pillows. They lay on special mattresses. They weren't sick. They were crumbling. Decaying. Eaten away by time. They were demonstrating the arcane art of perfect vanishing. Like stones that it's futile to seek on ragged shores. That was what Henryk's poem said about them.

The residents decayed rapidly.

Covered in boils. Spots. Blemishes. Scabs. Furrows. Drooling. Sweating. Panting. Trembling. Whimpering. Looking for who knows what. Groaning. Plodding from here to there. And back again, moth-eaten, toothless tigers in a cage. Fidgeting. Waiting for someone at the gate. Pestering the caregivers. Refusing to leave the treatment room. Moaning. Revealing their illnesses as if making a declaration of faith. Gripping their orthopedic sticks. Shoving along their walking frames. Striding without a handhold. They looked as if they were creeping up on someone or something. They hid pills under their tongues. Exhaled with a whistle. Toyed with their saliva. Broke wind. Corroded. Blistered. Ate away at themselves. Bodies ever bonier. Fleshless. Flabby. Cold. Their gluttony was clandestine, only practiced in solitude, in hiding. They were ashamed of their clumsy fingers. Straightened their legs diligently. Bent their knees carefully. Placed their feet cautiously. Plunged their fingers in the goo on their plates. Overcame their dizzy turns. Defeated their loss of balance. Drowned in pulmonary discharge. Wobbled down to the garden. Hastened ahead. Composed themselves. Endlessly. Coolly. As if trying to shield their mouths with a hand to avoid screaming.

Visits by relatives were a rare occurrence. Especially during the summer holidays. But Henryk's wife came to fetch him. She came onto the terrace. A second woman, younger, stayed by the car, afraid to approach the assembled residents.

Who's that woman over there? Henryk asked his wife.

Miłka, your adopted daughter.

And who are you?

Your wife, don't you remember me anymore? That's a good one.

You look like my mother. I'm not going with you. No.

But that lady has your newspaper knife at home. Really, the caregiver tried to persuade Henryk.

I've got your ivory-handled knife. Exotic. And very foreign, darling, mocked Henryk's wife, laughing.

Henryk believed her. He went away on holiday. Everyone envied him. Until they found out Henryk had been taken to the house by the lake. So said Miron. He'd overheard the caregivers' conversation.

The *Licuala grandis* had withered.

Leon tried to help it, despite the rule about saving water he always smuggled in one or two extra mugs for it. But its leaves were dropping off, and its stem was shrinking, becoming brittle. Finally Leon realized the end had come. The caregivers helped him to pull the plant out of its pot. He wrapped it in an old newspaper and laid it in a shallow pit. In the garden, under a sickly apple tree.

Bożydar watched as Leon raked the earth.

I can understand someone burying a mongrel. But a weed?

In what way is it inferior to a dog? Well, in what way? said Helena irritably.

Don't worry, maybe now the manager will let you have a dog. He's sure to agree to a very small one, said Leokadia to console Leon as she led him onto the terrace.

I don't want a dog anymore. Just think, what would become of it when I die? What would become of it?

He fell silent.

He hid his head in his arms. He stared vacantly ahead as the setting sun painted the gate the color of rust.

Miron began to fidget restlessly.

Can you feel it? A breeze, right? The Consul was right. The sea. The sea. You can smell the sea, can't you? he inquired, struggling to swallow his saliva.

There's no sea here, said Helena.

You can't smell anything. Nothing, concluded Miron, helplessly.

He nestled into a corner of the blanket thrown over the plastic chairs.

I'm not going to bargain for life, oh no. When my head starts to ache, I won't even ask for a tablet, declared Bożydar, counting up the signatures in his notebook.

I want to go to my eternal rest like a real he-man. Like going off to war, wholeheartedly, with strength, not like some puny runt. There's so much unhappiness in the world. It's a shame to die of old age. Will you sign? A petition about reducing the drugs. They're turning us into addicts.

I've already signed, squeaked Leokadia.

She appeared to be in a good mood, watching the dear little beetles and sparrows, but in fact she'd been holding back her tears all day. She had a sudden desire to go back to her room. She was sure she could reach the toilet in time. But her armchair sucked her in, and refused to let her go. Her body was betraying her by pretending to be asleep. She asked a caregiver for help. She asked in a mutter. She started a sentence. Then started it again. For some strange reason, she could only speak two or three words before something cut off her thoughts. She couldn't go on. The caregiver hadn't heard. Leokadia kept trying to ask. Finally she gave up, waving a hand.

She struggled to get up from her chair. At that point her bowels gushed forth. She fell onto the terrace. On her stomach. She vomited bile, stringy, like egg white. She was wallowing in it. Drowning. Gagging. Surfacing. Drowning. She couldn't turn her head. She had less and less sensation. She was rolling internally. Like a guillotined head. She was smeared in a coating of entrails. Of herself. She gasped for air. She felt a hand pulling her from the puke—like a blind puppy from a bucket of water to check if it has stopped breathing.

Miron was resting on a sticky bed.

He was clutching an ivory-handled knife. An unusual one. Exotic. He'd spotted a spider hooked to the ceiling. Its bulging abdomen was covered in rough bristles. It looked warm.

That afternoon, when Miron waddled off to have gentian painted on his gums, the spider had disappeared.

At bedtime the nurse brought his medicine.

Please calm down, she scolded Miron.

His trembling hands were avidly looting the room.

Now what's gone missing? she asked, displeased by the scattered clothes, and the back numbers of *Junior Modelmaker* and *Winged Poland*.

Miron spread his hands. He couldn't remember.

He stuck out his tongue, as if to receive the Host. Like a good boy, he swallowed the pill.

Once the nurse had left, he propped himself on raised arms against the door frame. He thought about the Sunday that had never actually come, when he had taken his son on a flight over Warsaw. When the roar of the engines had silenced the boy's laughter. Huddled against the wind, side by side, holding hands, they'd gone closer and closer to the machine. So large it couldn't possibly soar up into the sky a moment later.

Leon went out only rarely now.

For hours at a time he lay in bed. He hadn't the strength to go down to the terrace. He gazed at the ceiling. Ran his tongue over his lips. They were chapped, as if by a layer of salt.

The manager came to see him. He brought a chair up to the bed. And sat down.

Leon, we're reviewing your request. In the fall there'll be a doggie. Just a small one. You're pleased, right?

Yes, I am.

You speak very softly. No one can understand.

Thank you very much. Thank you for everything. My wife wanted to have a dog. Very much. And always from a shelter. During the war there was such awful poverty at her home in the countryside. She ate dogs.

All right, all right, You don't have to talk. I can't understand you anyway. The point is that in a month or two you'll have your doggie.

Thank you very much. I wish you all the best, said Leon.

He closed his eyes. He couldn't see any difference. He felt as if it were dark everywhere.

Leon had only felt all right in the camp. Before coming here he had visited the camp once a year. He'd say he was going on a business trip. Neither his wife nor his son knew anything about Leon's past. If you eat venom, you're poisoned, he excused himself.

He'd stay at a modest hotel in downtown Oświęcim. He'd spend two days walking around the camp. Sometimes he failed to reach the toilet in time. He'd vomit up memories. Wherever.

Every year he approached the camp administrator with the same question: Where was his bunk? In reply he was invariably told that it was being conserved. With a tired but patient look, as if Leon wasn't the only person who bothered the administration with this question.

The summer was losing its intensity.

The light was becoming subtle. Tangible. It didn't burn. The sky was dense with azure, like oil paint flooding a ceiling.

Miron had the best room. From the window he could see the gravel drive and the tall gate armed with the eye of a camera that was never switched on. He never closed the curtains. Not even in the greatest heat. He was always looking at the same spot.

Being in his room felt like being at a hotel. Every time he entered it, he had a strange sense of alienation; whatever the time of year he was always cold, and didn't know what to do. He lay there. His head was ajumble. Brightness and darkness. By turns. He squeezed his eyes shut. The colors were disintegrating. Faster and faster. Brightness, darkness.

He began to weep. Internally. Soundlessly. He sniffed, as if trying to restrain a cold. He caught a scent of mushroom spawn, of amber stubble fields, the prattling of children, the merry barking of dogs. He heard someone opening a door, and then shutting it soon after.

They say there are places on Earth where there are thirty-eight kinds of wild orchid and nineteen species of bee. Isn't that marvelous, mused Leokadia.

She was waiting for a bed on wheels to be found for her. They were moving her into the corridor. Apparently it was cooler there, and the nurse would be able to keep an eye on her, said Helena, trying to convince her.

Leokadia was afraid they wanted to wheel her off to the house by the lake. She wasn't eating. She was wilting, fading, consuming herself. She lay without moving, pressed into the bedclothes, immobile, but even so everything was still happening, relentlessly, without respite. Under her skin, inside her body.

She was waiting. Like a wounded, bleeding animal that's looking at the person removing it from a snare, but remains indifferent, resigned to pain, expecting nothing.

She was waiting for Helena, who wasn't coming. Had she managed to get past the gate yesterday? wondered Leokadia. Maybe she was already walking in the forest? Or lying with her head in the moss, sniffing the fungal dampness, as she used to do on their way back to the orphanage from school.

Leokadia strained her ears. She lay silently. With her mouth wide open. Her eyes staring. Alert. Tense. She looked as if she were being scooped up by an alien force, not external, but one that came from inside her, was born in her body, and was growing there, quietly, unhurriedly, imperceptibly. It was reaching, looting, cutting, slitting every cell of her body, every molecule. It was growing. Intensifying. Though the moment of its victory was quiet, noiseless, devoid of time.

Bożydar looked in on her. He saw that they'd put Leokadia in a bed on wheels. Oh dear, oh dear, he thought. He'd come to have her sign his petition about cooling drinks. He'd started collecting signatures after lunch today. As soon as the manager had announced that he was refusing their collective request for showers and shampoo.

Thank you very much. Thank you for coming, squeaked Leokadia, gazing at the ceiling.

Bożydar left without a word.

She felt the desire to go for a walk. Roll in the grass. Watch the sparrows hopping onto sheets of air.

She moved. Only a little, so it seemed to her, but she fell off the bed. She was pleased she had so much strength. Enough strength to crawl under the bed. Cling to the wall. Pull up her legs. Clamp her arms around her knees. An animal seeking relief.

At two twenty in the morning Leokadia was standing in line for the slaughterhouse for patient old beasts of burden.

With difficulty, on their knees, the caregivers pulled her out from under the bed. They laid her on a plastic sheet thrown over the bedding. Her head sank deep into the pillow. Weighed down by orthopedic boots, her feet hung over the floor. She looked as if she had just meant to lie down a while, when suddenly, to her own surprise, she had turned to stone.

They opened a window. One of the caregivers went to call the doctor and the Kiss of Eden. A volunteer lit a Paschal candle outside the door into Leokadia's room. Gradually the residents came together.

Helena stood quietly in a corner of the room. Finally she went up to the bed, knelt down, and took off her sister's shoes. She lost her balance. She reeled. Clung to the bed rails. She felt the pressure of the metal bars against her chest, a good pain that let her do less thinking. She struggled to her feet. And rested with her eyes closed.

Then she laid the dead woman's feet on the bedding. They were very thin, astonishingly heavy. She sat down on the edge of the bed. She stroked her sister's hair and cheek, and warmed her hands in her own. She gazed at the face, she couldn't take her eyes off it.

The night was short, violent, marked by a hailstorm.

Helena plodded to the window, leaned against the sill, and looked into dark space.

Parched by the heat of the sun, the throat of summer was greedily drinking. Sucking. The wind was hurling rain mixed with hail and sand at the windowpanes. The water struck hard, steadily. It was splashing in the gutters. Spilling over the sill. Advancing further. Spreading. Collecting under the leaky window ledge. Getting inside. In drops, threads, offshoots, streams. Forcing its way under the sill. Under her hands.

Hailstones struck Helena in the face, pressing their way inside. She could turn them in her mouth, hold them under her tongue, and roll them between her lips.

The day was slowly dawning when she went downstairs and into the garden. The crowns of the trees were shining with moisture as they unhurriedly shook off the downpour. Bruised and nipped by the hail, the leaves were tautening. The saturated air had revived brown centipedes, dark-blue beetles, and worms teeming in the drenched grass.

She went out beyond the gate. At once she came off the road, went into the bushes, and on, into the forest. No one called after her. She walked with effort. Her shoes sank into the wet forest floor. Leaves, tufts of grass, and conifer needles stuck to them.

She saw a black car. There was a man asleep on the hood. With his head among calla lilies. Beaded with moisture. She thought his body looked young and juicy. More animal than human. She stopped.

The man opened his eyes and didn't show surprise. He sat up, and nodded by way of greeting. Slowly, he shook off sleep.

I'm not crumpled, am I? asked Helena, turning on her own axis.

They say you're a snappy dresser. All spick and span, he replied.

She smiled.

Ah, so you know all about me? I was Miss Auschwitz. Little Miss Auschwitz. They wanted to look at me day after day. All the time. Non-stop. I could be displayed. Shown off. Gripped by the face to demonstrate my peachy skin, my lack of scabies and scabs with gorged lice. Shown and preserved. Kept as a memento. Just like souvenirs of journeys: if they're lovely, the trip must have been beautiful too. I'm not crumpled, am I? she asked, neatening her pantsuit.

He was silent.

Well, why don't you say something? You're surprised? No, nothing surprises you anymore, does it? Only doctors and whores are never surprised, that's what my husband used to say. *Ja, gut,* not in front of people, of course. Only when we were alone, the two of us. *Gut, gut.*

Helena broke off.

With a slow, weary gesture she smoothed the material on her hips.

Do you remember me? he asked after a while.

Ah, so it's you.

She looked at him more closely. Clean-shaven, hair clipped very close to his skull, and prominent cheekbones gave his face an exotic look. One of his eyebrows was bisected by a short scar. She went closer and touched that spot.

What's this mark? she asked, holding her fingertip to the man's skin for too long.

One of the stiffs bit me. Sometimes I end up transporting vampires.

He burst out laughing.

It's a scar from childhood, she said matter-of-factly.

I can tell if a flaw on the skin is temporary and will heal, or is old, there forever.

He stopped laughing. As if he'd lost patience.

Apparently the dead don't touch, she said, wanting to fill the man's silence.

That's why you like your work so much, isn't it?

He didn't answer.

She looked around.

After the hailstorm it had suddenly become cool. The summer was ending. At last.

I'm sorry I didn't bring a sweater. I have a favorite one. Wine-red. It suits me well. It casts a nice glow. Rejuvenates. In certain colors one simply looks younger, don't you think? Ah, so it's the end of the summer. Henryk was right, I can feel the breeze. The crisp air. Who'd have thought, such a big hailstorm at this time of year, said Helena, smiling.

She turned around and started walking straight ahead, toward the city. She went a few yards.